Every inch a

Ashleigh rode Glory by the stands in the post parade. Cindy admired the finely bred Thoroughbred almost as if he wasn't hers. With generations of winners in his pedigree, he looked every inch a champion. She saw with relief that the noise and distractions from the stands didn't faze the big colt, even when a paper bag sailed lazily onto the track a few inches from his hooves.

Cindy's stomach calmed a little, then twisted again when Glory balked going into the starting gate. Ashleigh sat quietly. A gate attendant tugged on Glory's bridle, and the colt reluctantly loaded.

A rainbow appeared, arching high over the starting gate and disappearing into the hills. The sky was clearing to the west, turning a pale, clean-washed blue.

"I never saw *that* before at a race," Samantha said, pointing to the rainbow.

"It's a perfect rainbow," Cindy said happily. "Not just a half one, the way they sometimes are."

"I'll bet you're thinking this is an omen that Glory will win." Mike chuckled.

"I *know* it is," Cindy said.

Collect all the books in the Thoroughbred series

#1 *A Horse Called Wonder*
#2 *Wonder's Promise*
#3 *Wonder's First Race*
#4 *Wonder's Victory*
#5 *Ashleigh's Dream*
#6 *Wonder's Yearling*
#7 *Samantha's Pride*
#8 *Sierra's Steeplechase*
#9 *Pride's Challenge*
#10 *Pride's Last Race*
#11 *Wonder's Sister*
#12 *Shining's Orphan*
#13 *Cindy's Runaway Colt*
#14 *Cindy's Glory*
#15 *Glory's Triumph*
#16 *Glory in Danger*
#17 *Ashleigh's Farewell*
#18 *Glory's Rival*
#19 *Cindy's Heartbreak*
#20 *Champion's Spirit*
#21 *Wonder's Champion*
#22 *Arabian Challenge*
#23 *Cindy's Honor*
#24 *The Horse of Her Dreams*
#25 *Melanie's Treasure*
#26 *Sterling's Second Chance*
#27 *Christina's Courage*
#28 *Camp Saddlebrook*
#29 *Melanie's Last Ride*
#30 *Dylan's Choice*
#31 *A Home for Melanie*
#32 *Cassidy's Secret*
#33 *Racing Parker*
#34 *On the Track*
#35 *Dead Heat*
#36 *Without Wonder*
#37 *Star in Danger*
#38 *Down to the Wire*
#39 *Living Legend*
#40 *Ultimate Risk*
#41 *Close Call*
#42 *The Bad-Luck Filly*
#43 *Fallen Star*
#44 *Perfect Image*
#45 *Star's Chance*
#46 *Racing Image*
#47 *Cindy's Desert Adventure*
#48 *Cindy's Bold Start*
#49 *Rising Star*
#50 *Team Player*
#51 *Distance Runner*
#52 *Perfect Challenge*
#53 *Derby Fever*
#54 *Cindy's Last Hope*
#55 *Great Expectations*
#56 *Hoofprints in the Snow**

Collect all the books in the Ashleigh series

#1 *Lightning's Last Hope*
#2 *A Horse for Christmas*
#3 *Waiting for Stardust*
#4 *Good-bye, Midnight Wanderer*
#5 *The Forbidden Stallion*
#6 *A Dangerous Ride*
#7 *Derby Day*
#8 *The Lost Foal*
#9 *Holiday Homecoming*
#10 *Derby Dreams*
#11 *Ashleigh's Promise*
#12 *Winter Race Camp*
#13 *The Prize*
#14 *Ashleigh's Western Challenge**

THOROUGHBRED Super Editions
Ashleigh's Christmas Miracle
Ashleigh's Diary
Ashleigh's Hope
Samantha's Journey

ASHLEIGH'S Thoroughbred Collection
Star of Shadowbrook Farm
The Forgotten Filly
Battlecry Forever!

coming soon*

THOROUGHBRED

Glory's Triumph

WRITTEN BY
KAREN BENTLEY

CREATED BY
JOANNA CAMPBELL

HarperPaperbacks
A Division of HarperCollins*Publishers*

This is a work of fiction. The characters, incidents, and dialogues are products of the author's imagination and are not to be construed as real. Any resemblance to actual events or persons, living or dead, is entirely coincidental.

HarperPaperbacks *A Division of* HarperCollins*Publishers*
10 East 53rd Street, New York, N.Y. 10022

First printing: January 1996

Printed in the United States of America

HarperPaperbacks and colophon are trademarks of HarperCollins*Publishers*

❖ 10 9 8 7

For John

Glory's Triumph

"GLORY, IT'S ONLY A BIRD." CINDY MCLEAN LAUGHED AND leaned forward in the saddle to pat the Thoroughbred's sleek neck. "At least I *think* that's what you're scared of."

The big gray colt snorted and crabstepped, his breath misting in the cool late February air. Then he stopped dead on the trail to stare at a large oak. On one of the top branches a brown bird had just landed with a flutter of wings. The bird gave a small, fierce cry.

"Okay," Cindy said, settling back in the saddle. *Glory really does spook a lot, from almost everything,* she thought. *But I'll train that out of him with a lot of work—and love.* "Take a look for as long as you want," she urged. "But that bird isn't going to bite you."

Glory tossed his elegant gray head and snorted.

"He doesn't believe you," Heather Gilbert called as she trotted up on Bo Jangles. Heather was Cindy's best friend and usually rode Bo on the trails with Cindy at Whitebrook. Cindy's adoptive father, Ian McLean, was head trainer at the breeding and training farm just outside Lexington.

"He'll calm down," Cindy said. "He just needs to get completely used to the trails." She ran her hand lovingly along Glory's muscular shoulder. The sunlight streaming through the bare winter branches added more patches of light and dark to his dappled coat.

Cindy kept her other hand firmly on the reins. She had been riding Glory over the trails at Whitebrook for about six weeks now, and she knew he could be unpredictable.

Suddenly Glory seemed to make up his mind not to let the bird bother him. With a final snort he walked on, sidestepping just a little as they went by the tree.

"Good boy. You can do anything if you try." Cindy let the reins slide through her fingers a little and breathed in the faint, cold scent of melting snow that lingered in the late February air. Glory was moving along the trail now, his gait light and springy, tossing his head with pleasure. He seemed to be enjoying the gorgeous late winter day as much as Cindy was.

"Ugh!" Heather shook her light blond hair. "A big blob of melting snow just dropped off that branch on me. I'm getting tired of cold weather."

"I'm not, really," Cindy said. "The horses seem to love it—they're always friskier in the winter. The only bad thing is that when they race at this time of year, it's always someplace warm and far away, like Florida or California. Then I usually can't go to watch because of school. But in just a couple of weeks I will be in California," Cindy added excitedly. "I'll see Shining race in the Santa Anita Handicap."

"I know." Heather grinned. "You've told me twelve times already."

"Have I? I can't stop thinking about it—it's an incredibly important race for Shining and Samantha." Cindy smiled, thinking about the big red roan mare that Samantha, her eighteen-year-old adoptive sister, had trained from a scraggly, sick horse into a champion. Cindy was Shining's groom.

"I wouldn't mind going to California," Heather said as she leaned down in the saddle to adjust a stirrup.

"It's going to be great. I'll be twelve next month, but I've never even been out of Kentucky," Cindy said. "And I've never been on a plane, either."

"Will you get to miss school?" Heather asked.

Cindy knew Heather wasn't crazy about school. She was very creative and did well in art class, but she was too shy to enjoy being around most people. Heather and Cindy had become instant friends last year in school through their love of horses.

"I'll fly there the Friday before the race and then be back Sunday night. So I won't miss any school." Cindy frowned. She wouldn't mind missing some school right now either. That wasn't usually the case. Cindy enjoyed learning new things, and her grades were excellent.

Enter Max Smith, Cindy thought sourly. Max was one of the most popular boys in her sixth-grade class, but for some reason he didn't like her. Yesterday he'd embarrassed her in front of the whole class when he'd stuck out a foot and tried to trip her, almost making her fall flat on her face.

Glory tugged on the reins, reminding Cindy of more important things than Max. "Let's canter," she said. "Glory needs a real workout."

"He's going into training soon, right?" Heather asked.

"He starts tomorrow. If it goes well, he could race in the late spring. Can you believe how far he's come since we were hiding him in the shed?" Last September, Cindy had found Glory loose in the woods, running in terror from the two men who had stolen him from his first owner, then cruelly abused him. To keep them from finding Glory, she'd fixed up a vacant shed for him at Whitebrook. Only Heather had known he was there.

"Yeah, it seems like just yesterday we were sneaking hay and grain to him." Heather ran her hand along Bo's mane.

"I was so afraid I'd have to give him back to those mean men," Cindy said with a sigh. Eventually she, Heather, and Glory had gotten caught hiding out. Cindy could smile about it now.

"What?" Heather asked.

"I guess it was pretty hard to hide a twelve-hundred-pound horse," Cindy said. "He didn't exactly fit in my pocket!"

Cindy's parents had tried to return Glory to his actual owner, but by then the man had been killed in a car accident. Glory was put up for sale as part of the estate, and Whitebrook had bought him as a potential racehorse at the Keeneland winter auction in January. Cindy's adoption papers, making her officially one of the McLeans, had been finalized at almost the same time Glory came to Whitebrook.

Glory and I both got adopted, Cindy thought happily. She lightly touched Glory's sides with her heels, cueing him to canter.

The big Thoroughbred needed no further encouragement. He flung up his head and tried to break into a gallop.

"Take it easy, boy," Cindy told him, pulling hard on the reins. "Save it for the track. This is just exercise."

Glory fought her briefly, then realized she meant business and settled into a smooth, rocking canter.

The cold breeze lifted Cindy's hair and brought a flush to her cheeks. A smile of absolute bliss came to her face. She couldn't imagine a life better than this—sitting deep in the saddle, with the rhythmic, easy strides of the powerful Thoroughbred eating up the ground beneath her. Glory was in excellent condition from the trail ride Cindy gave him almost every day. His breath hardly misted the air.

Suddenly Glory shied again, ducking sideways off the trail and breaking into a nervous, high-stepping trot. Cindy tightened her legs to keep her seat. The big gray's ears pricked forward.

"What is it?" Cindy asked patiently.

Glory settled down, responding to Cindy's soothing tone. In the quiet Cindy could hear a faint crackling of brush. The next moment Ashleigh Griffen and her husband, Mike Reese, rode around a bend in the trail. Mike and Ashleigh had been good friends for years and had married the summer before last.

"Hey, guys," Ashleigh said, pulling up Sagebrush, a compact two-year-old in training for the spring races. The chestnut colt stopped obediently.

"Hi," Heather said, looking over at Sagebrush. Bo Jangles sensed she wasn't paying attention and snatched a mouthful from an evergreen bush.

"Stop it!" Heather said indignantly, hauling him back with the reins. Bo chomped contentedly.

"Is he being a terror?" Mike asked with a laugh. He was riding Polar Danzig, a light gray two-year-old colt also in training.

"Not really. It's just that Sasha's a little easier to handle," Heather said, referring to the easygoing bay filly she rode in her jumping lessons.

"How's Glory going?" Ashleigh asked.

"Just perfectly," Cindy said fondly, rubbing Glory's small, finely shaped ears. Glory craned his head around to nudge her boot.

"Looks like he thinks you're a perfect rider." Ashleigh laughed.

That's a better description of you, Cindy thought. When Ashleigh was just sixteen, she won the Breeders' Cup Classic on Ashleigh's Wonder, a horse she had helped raise and train. Now twenty-two, Ashleigh owned Whitebrook with Mike and his father, Gene Reese.

"No more problems with shying?" Ashleigh asked.

"A little," Cindy admitted.

"Well, keep working with him." Ashleigh looked at Glory, her hazel eyes thoughtful.

"He just needs time," Mike said encouragingly.

Cindy bit her lip. Mike was right, but Glory definitely wasn't always an angel. She just couldn't tell Ashleigh how much Glory did spook, or that a couple of times he'd almost unseated her.

"We've got to get back to the stable to feed," Ashleigh said. "See you later." She and Mike turned their horses and trotted them down the trail.

"We'd better go back too," Cindy said to Heather. "We have to cool out the horses before they eat."

"Yeah, and I've got to start my homework," Heather said.

The setting sun touched the hills to the west as they walked the horses out of the woods. Below, the day's last light turned the Reeses' white-painted farmhouse and the McLeans' cottage to gold. The training, stallion, and broodmare barns, usually deep red in color, glowed dusky orange.

"I wish Glory would stop this spooking business," Cindy said worriedly.

"There's so much we don't know about him," Heather said. "He might have bad memories from when he was stolen."

"Yeah." Cindy frowned, squinting into the sun as they walked the horses along the lane between the paddocks. "I'm sure Ashleigh and Samantha will do a fantastic job training him. I mean, look at how Wonder and Shining turned out."

"I guess you'd settle for another Breeders' Cup winner, like Wonder," Heather said seriously.

"Maybe." Cindy grinned. "But I really have my heart set on Horse of the Year." Suddenly she laughed and pointed to the side paddock. "Look at Mr. Wonderful!"

Wonder's two-year-old chestnut son cantered up to the fence. His whiskers were frosted with a last bit of snow he'd found to play in.

Heather laughed too. "Will he race this year?" she asked.

Cindy nodded. "That's the plan—in April, at Keeneland. He's already in training."

As the girls rode into the stable yard, Cindy thought again about Glory's training. Of course it would be exciting to watch Ashleigh and Samantha train Glory. They had a lot of experience, and they'd bring out the best of him on the track.

But I want to exercise ride him and train him, Cindy thought as she dismounted and pulled up her stirrups. She knew it wasn't a realistic hope. Exercise riding and training a Thoroughbred took a lot of skill, and Cindy had been riding horses for just six months. And she was only eleven—that was young even to be a groom.

"How was your ride?" Len, the old stable manager, greeted the girls. He took Glory's reins.

"Excellent." Cindy felt her smile return. She rubbed Glory's neck.

"This big horse couldn't look better," Len remarked. "I'll untack him—do you want to cool him out?"

"Sure. I'll get his feed ready and be back in a second."

"I'll untack Bo and we'll meet you out front," Heather said.

Cindy carefully measured out Glory's feed, vitamins, and minerals in the feed room and carried the full bucket to his feed box. Just outside the barn, Len had put a light blanket on the colt. Cindy took Glory's lead rope from the stable manager and began to slowly circle the stable yard with Heather and Bo Jangles.

After she was sure Glory was completely cooled out, Cindy put him in his roomy box stall. Imp, the colt's faithful gray cat companion, hopped up on the stall door and began a meticulous bath. The young horse eagerly pushed his muzzle deep into his feed and munched happily.

"Good stuff, huh?" Cindy asked.

"Nothing wrong with his appetite," Len said, coming up outside the stall and looking in on them. "The new vet's going to check him over, though, when she comes out in a couple of days to look at Blues King's leg—he's got a bad infection that won't clear up. Ashleigh wants to make sure Glory's coming along okay with exercise."

Heather popped her head over the half door to Glory's stall. The colt gave a surprised snort and shied. "Oh, sorry, big guy," Heather said.

Glory nervously turned around several times in his stall. Imp stopped washing his paw and stared with accusing green eyes at Heather.

Cindy laid a soothing hand on Glory's shoulder until the horse had stopped fidgeting. "No one's come to kidnap you," she said.

Glory's ears flicked back. He stepped over to his feed box and snatched a bite.

"I put Bo in his stall," Heather said. "My mom's here. I'd better get going—I've got that huge science project to start. It's already Tuesday, and we've got to turn it in Friday."

"Okay. See you tomorrow at school." Cindy had already finished her science project. She didn't want to go up to the house until after she said good night to all the horses. Since they were in three different barns, that was going to take a while. Tonight Cindy especially wanted to visit Wonder.

Glory had calmed down and was cleaning up the last bits of grain from his box. He looked the picture of a healthy, contented horse.

"Good night, beautiful," Cindy said, dropping a kiss on Glory's black nose. "Sleep well. Tomorrow is your first day in training. You've got to do your very best."

Glory looked at her and bobbed his head, apparently agreeing.

The dim night-lights were on in the broodmare barn as Cindy walked down the aisle to Wonder's stall. Whitebrook's five mares in foal had finished their grain, and Cindy could hear the quiet rustle as the mares pulled mouthfuls of hay from the sheaves. Wonder was in a stall at the middle of the barn.

Cindy peeked over the stall door. "Hey, gorgeous," she said softly. "How's it going?"

Wonder looked up from her hay net. Cindy's breath caught in her throat, then she slowly let it out. Wonder's brilliant copper coat gleamed in the soft barn lights. Cindy knew the champion mare had perfect conformation. Wonder's powerful quarters, deep chest, and straight legs had made her first at the wire in the biggest races. *Wonder always wanted to win when she raced,* Cindy thought. *You can tell how much heart she has just from her eyes.*

The chestnut mare stepped over to the stall door, dropped her elegant head, and sniffed Cindy's hands. Wonder was in foal to Townsend Victor. She would deliver sometime in April.

"Are you going to have another champion like Pride?" Cindy asked, stroking Wonder's soft muzzle. "I'll bet you are." Wonder's Pride, Wonder's first foal, had won many big stakes races and been Horse of the Year. Now he was at stud at Whitebrook.

"I can't believe I'm standing here patting your nose, Wonder." Cindy smiled. "Aren't you too important for that?" Wonder was a legend in Kentucky as a racehorse and a broodmare.

Cindy narrowed her eyes, imagining the days when Wonder had raced. Ashleigh had often told Cindy about those times. She could almost hear the announcer at Churchill Downs: *And they're into the stretch. Townsend Prince and Mercy Man are running nose to nose, straining to catch Ashleigh's Wonder. But the filly has been asked for more, and she's giving it! Ashleigh's Wonder has won the Kentucky Derby. . . .*

But Wonder hadn't always been a miracle horse, Cindy reminded herself. Wonder had gotten off to a rough start, just like Glory. She'd been a sickly foal and almost died. For years only Ashleigh had any confidence in her.

The mare went back to her dinner. *You never know,* Cindy said to herself. *Maybe Glory will be the next major champion on this farm.*

A DELICIOUS-SMELLING, WARM WAVE HIT CINDY THE instant she opened the McLeans' cottage door. Cindy sniffed appreciatively. "What's for dinner?" she called as she tugged off her boots in the hall.

Beth McLean, Ian's wife and an aerobics instructor, poked her head out of the kitchen, a spatula in her hand. "Broiled salmon steaks," she said. "And New York style cheesecake for dessert."

"Wow. I'm starved." Cindy walked into the kitchen and took a celery stick from a plate of vegetables and dip on the table.

"I can think of worse things than having a mother who's a gourmet cook," Samantha McLean said, grinning. She joined Cindy at the table.

Beth looked pleased. Cindy remembered that Samantha had told her she had only recently begun to think of Beth as her mother. Ian and Beth had married about a year ago.

Ian turned from the kitchen counter. "The cheesecake's my contribution."

"Sometime will you teach me how to make it?" Cindy asked.

"Sure, honey." Ian carefully opened the oven door to check on the golden brown cheesecake.

"Let's be careful we don't get too carried away with fattening foods," Beth cautioned. "Eating a rich dessert like cheesecake once a week is probably enough." Beth was scrupulous about healthy diets.

Blond, handsome Tor Nelson, Samantha's longtime steady boyfriend, stood next to Ian, rinsing the mixer beaters. "Hey, Cindy," he said. "I just saw Heather leaving. How'd she do on Bo?"

"She likes Sasha better." Cindy ran a carrot around the edge of the dip bowl, collecting the last bit of the spicy mix.

"Jumpers are my favorite kind of horse too," Tor said with a laugh. Tor and his father owned a jumping stable in Lexington, and Tor competed in jumping on the national level. He gave Heather lessons in exchange for her cleaning tack and doing other stable chores.

"Dinner's ready," Beth announced.

They all sat at the kitchen table and helped themselves to portions of steaming salmon.

"Where have you been hiding yourself, Tor?" Ian asked.

"Good question." Samantha raised an eyebrow and looked sideways at her boyfriend.

"I've been buried alive." Tor reached for the bottle of mineral water. "I'd have plenty to do if I had just my jumping classes to teach and college. But on top of that I'm trying to get Sierra in shape for the spring steeplechases and train High Caliber, my new jumper, for summer shows. So I haven't had time for a lot of the things I'd like to do." He gave Samantha an apologetic smile. "Do you think you could take Sierra over some jumps tomorrow while I coach you?"

I'm glad he didn't ask me, Cindy thought, taking a gulp of milk. Tor had taught Cindy how to jump a little on one of his school horses, but Sierra was another story. Cindy knew, though, that despite Sierra's difficult temperament and dismal performance at flat racing, he was a great steeplechaser.

"I'll work Sierra tomorrow when I come over for the Pony Commandos' lesson," Samantha said, returning Tor's smile. "But don't try to tell me you're busier than I am. I've got classes, and even more horses to work than you." Samantha was a freshman at the University of Kentucky. Tor was in his junior year.

"I know," Tor said. He squeezed her hand. "Cindy, can you come over too and help out?"

"Sure, Heather and I both will." For the past few months Cindy and Heather had assisted Tor and Samantha with the riding class they taught for six disabled children.

"Great," Tor said, sounding relieved. "I'll have a surprise for everybody at the lesson. I've been doing a little course design. Not only for my advanced jumpers, but for the Commandos too. Some of those kids are really coming along—especially Mandy Jarvis."

"She's definitely the best in the class," Cindy agreed. "I bet she could even compete with kids who aren't disabled." Mandy wore leg braces from her ankles to her knees, the result of a car accident three years ago, when she was five. She had become an excellent rider through determination and talent. Cindy had liked the spirited girl from the moment they'd met.

"I sometimes forget the effort Mandy puts into her riding," Samantha said. "She has to overcome her physical problems, then show extra ability to shine. She's really amazing."

"She is," Tor agreed. "The Commandos will be over at five tomorrow—can you make it then?"

"We'll be there right after we feed the horses. I have one fewer horse to take care of since Shining's away, but I wish I could be with her." Samantha's prize mare had been in California for several weeks, running in winter races at the Santa Anita track in Los Angeles.

"She's doing fine," Ian said. "Her win in the San Antonio Handicap last week was decisive."

"But the Santa Anita Handicap is in just three weeks, and Shining's going up against a lot stiffer competition. You know we're running against Her Majesty again," Samantha said.

"Oh, no." Cindy groaned. "Not another matchup with the Townsends!" Clay Townsend was the owner of Townsend Acres, a huge breeding and training farm just outside Lexington. He and Ashleigh were co-owners of Wonder and all her offspring. Mr. Townsend was all right, Cindy supposed, although he and Ashleigh had certainly had their differences, especially when Wonder's Pride was racing.

But the real problem with the Townsends was Brad, Mr. Townsend's son. Handsome and arrogant, Brad was always trying to run Townsend Acres. And because Mr. Townsend was half-owner of Wonder, Wonder's Pride, and Mr. Wonderful, who were all stabled at Whitebrook, Brad was a constant, uninvited, irritating presence at Whitebrook too.

"Every time we come up against the Townsends, they do seem to make life unpleasant," Ian said.

Cindy made a face. That was an understatement. For a while the Townsends had made Cindy's life absolutely miserable when Brad's stuck-up wife, Lavinia, had accused Cindy of stealing a watch soon after she arrived at Whitebrook. Cindy had almost been sent to another foster home.

"I'm not too worried about Her Majesty." Samantha shrugged. "Shining's beaten her twice before."

"I'm not worried about the competition. I know Shining will beat every horse on the field," Cindy said. "It's the Townsends—they always cause trouble."

"Don't waste a lot of time thinking about the Townsends," Samantha said. "They're not worth it."

Cindy hoped Samantha was right. At least the Townsends couldn't cause problems with Glory—they didn't own any part of him.

"Cheesecake?" Beth asked Cindy, holding out the luscious-looking dessert on a round platter.

"Please." Cindy cut a slice and passed the platter. Everyone took a piece.

"This is fantastic, Ian," Tor said. "It's so creamy."

"Yeah, really." Cindy took another big bite.

"I'm taking Glory out tomorrow too." Samantha gave Cindy a thumbs-up across the table.

Cindy smiled back. Samantha seemed as thrilled as she was about Glory's prospects.

"A lot of big events are coming up," Beth said. "We really should start getting things together for our trip to the Santa Anita races. Cindy, we need to go shopping. You don't have any nice shorts or other lightweight clothes for the trip."

"Fine with me." Cindy didn't need to be persuaded. The dream trip to California was starting to seem real.

The next morning Cindy shivered in the chilly air as she walked to the training barn to start on her chores. The sun, pale and ghostly in the early sky, illuminated a veil of high, gray clouds as dappled as Glory's coat. Cindy's boots crunched on a light sprinkling of frost.

Glory greeted her with a delighted whinny. He leaned over the half-door of his stall and repeatedly tossed his handsome head.

"You're up and at 'em," Cindy told him. "I guess you're ready for breakfast."

Glory whinnied indignantly.

Cindy laughed and hurried to feed him the special

training ration of grain that Ashleigh had prescribed on his chart. Even switching Glory to the new diet was exciting, Cindy thought—he was being treated like a real racehorse!

"That's just what you're going to be," Cindy said, watching Glory relish his breakfast. At least she probably wouldn't have to worry about keeping his weight up while he was in training.

Ashleigh walked down the aisle to join her, clipboard in hand. "He's looking fit," she said. "While he finishes eating, why don't you come out and watch Mr. Wonderful's work? Samantha will ride him first, then she'll ride Glory. I'll take both of them around when we get closer to their races so I'll know what to expect on the big day."

Cindy's mouth dropped open. "*You're* going to ride Glory in his first race?"

Ashleigh smiled. "I was planning on it. Okay?"

"More than okay," Cindy managed to get out. "Incredible!"

"Well, Glory is a Whitebrook horse." Ashleigh reached over the stall door and ran a hand down Glory's satiny neck. "I've got an interest in his doing well."

"I'm glad you've got time to ride him," Cindy said happily. Now nothing could go wrong for Glory.

"I'll make time." Ashleigh continued down the aisle to Mr. Wonderful's stall. The chestnut colt had been fed earlier, and Len already had him groomed and ready to go.

"Morning, sweetie." Mr. McLean waved at Cindy from the doorway of the stable office. "Today's Glory's big day, huh?"

"Yeah—he's going out after Mr. Wonderful."

"Go for Glory!" Vic said as he passed her with an armload of leg wraps. Vic was the young full-time groom at Whitebrook.

Cindy grinned. Everyone was rooting for Glory—that was nice.

Cindy thoroughly groomed the big gray colt in his stall. Glory leaned into the brush strokes, enjoying the attention. "Don't fall asleep," Cindy warned. "This isn't just another day. You're not going out in the paddock to play and then take a nap in the sun. We've got work to do."

Glory huffed out a sigh. Cindy laughed and gave him one last pat. As she left the barn the colt was hanging his head out over the door, watching her.

Zipping up her jacket, Cindy walked over to the training oval rail and stood next to Ashleigh as Samantha rode Mr. Wonderful through the gap. The colt's honey-colored coat gleamed a subdued, rich chestnut under the gray sky. His powerful muscles, conditioned by longeing and trail rides, rippled as he walked up the track. He had really grown up over the winter, Cindy thought.

"Warm Mr. Wonderful up good, then breeze him out a quarter," Ashleigh called to Samantha. "He's doing so well, we just need to keep him right where he is until about a few weeks before the race. Then we'll step up his workouts a bit."

Samantha nodded and tightened the strap on her helmet.

Cindy watched intently as Samantha trotted and cantered Mr. Wonderful as a warmup, then galloped him toward the quarter pole. As many times as Cindy had seen workouts, she still felt a thrill when Samantha crouched over Mr. Wonderful's neck, signaling the horse to breeze out the last quarter. The colt was flying!

They flashed past the mile marker pole and Samantha stood in her stirrups. Mr. Wonderful gradually slowed, until finally Samantha had him back in a trot.

"What did you think?" Samantha asked, riding over to them. She took off her helmet and shook out her red hair.

"Do you need to ask? He's going great." Ashleigh waved her stopwatch and grinned. "Dream horse."

"That must be a wonderful feeling." Cindy sighed.

"It is and it isn't," Ashleigh said. "You're not really safe with a racehorse even at the top of the game. Things were going great for Wonder—until she fractured her cannon bone."

Cindy glanced at Samantha to see if this conversation was upsetting her. What about Shining? She could get hurt too. But Samantha looked composed.

"The vet said Wonder may not have really strong bones, and that's why she broke her leg," Ashleigh went on. "I think she just pounded the track for all she was worth in every race. Finally it would have been too much for any horse's legs."

"Aren't you scared for the horses when you ride?" Cindy asked. "I'm kind of afraid to even talk about it."

"The risk of horses getting injured is part of the racing business," Samantha said. "It's not something I think about much."

"Jockeys tend to get banged up too." Ashleigh grimaced. "Not my favorite subject. You're right, Cindy—let's not talk about all this. Ian's giving Polar Danzig just a light work this morning, and they'll be done in a minute. Then we'll have the track to ourselves. Why don't you bring out Glory, Cindy? We'll let him show his stuff."

"Sure." Cindy ran to the barn to get Glory, jumping over a couple of cavalletti near the path. Her heart was pounding with excitement. This was it, when Glory would show everyone his speed!

Glory was crosstied in the aisle. When he saw Cindy, he strained toward her against the ropes.

"He's all yours," Len said, unclipping him. "I tacked him up and got him ready for you."

"Thanks, Len." Cindy took Glory's reins from the stable manager.

"Watch him," Len said. "You know he can be a perfect gentleman, or—"

"He can explode," Cindy finished. "I'll be careful."

As if Glory had understood the discussion, just outside the barn he spooked, freezing stiff-legged, then skittering sideways. He almost yanked the reins out of Cindy's hand.

Instinctively Cindy tightened her grip and pulled

him back to her side. "Glory!" she scolded. "What's gotten into you?"

Glory flicked his ears, listening to Cindy's voice, but he was still prancing and crabstepping as she led him up to the oval. Oh, well, maybe he was just picking up on her excitement, she thought. He'd settle down in a minute.

Samantha didn't seem perturbed at the sight of the jittery colt. "He's raring to go," she commented. Cindy held Glory while Samantha mounted and adjusted her stirrups.

"Okay," Ashleigh said. "The first thing to do is find out where Glory already is in his training. He was a two-year-old when he was stolen, so he must have had some. Glory worked pretty well for you that one time you took him around last fall, Sammy, after Cindy's wild ride on him."

Cindy winced. Right after she'd found Glory, she'd wanted desperately to show everyone at Whitebrook how much talent he had, so that the farm would buy him at the Keeneland auction. Cindy had tried to breeze him around the track before either of them knew what they were doing. The ride had almost ended in disaster.

At least Ashleigh was out of town then, Cindy thought, glancing sideways at her. Cindy hoped that whatever story Ashleigh had heard about the episode with Glory wasn't the young trainer's only impression of her as a rider.

"Just trot him around, Samantha, and try to get a

sense of what he knows," Ashleigh said. "See if he leans into the rail or lugs out. If he knows to stay close to the rail, he's definitely been worked a decent amount on a track before."

Samantha signaled Glory to move out along the track. Cindy gripped the rail tightly. *Come on, Glory,* she willed him silently. *Put in another great work for Samantha.* Glory's black-and-gray mane and tail spilled behind him, turning silver in the overcast day. His steps were light and precise. He looked so beautiful, Cindy's throat ached.

Samantha put Glory into a trot, then a canter. Glory stayed right at the rail.

"He's definitely been on a track before," Ashleigh muttered. "He knows what's expected of him."

A cool breeze picked up, ruffling Cindy's blond hair. She pushed it out of her eyes and looked over at the track. Glory was leaping sideways, spooking. He was about to hit the rail! "Oh, no!" she cried. What would happen to Samantha if Glory went through the rail? Samantha's mother had been killed when a green horse she was riding did that!

Samantha reacted instantly, yanking on her right rein and trying to force Glory out to the center of the track. Glory resisted and lunged back toward the rail. For a second the colt's feet and head went in opposite directions. He stumbled and almost fell to his knees. Samantha pulled up Glory's head, and shakily the big colt found his footing again.

"Good," Cindy said. A second later she realized her

relief was premature. Glory seized the bit in his teeth and bolted.

What a nightmare, Cindy thought in horror as Glory pounded along the backstretch, throwing up his head, now totally out of control. *Why is he doing this?* Cindy squeezed the rail until her hands hurt. Ashleigh hadn't moved.

Samantha finally managed to stop Glory in the far corner of the track, but even from that distance Cindy could see he was trembling. Samantha was patting his neck and talking to him. Ashleigh motioned them to come back over to the gap.

"I wonder what he spooked from," Samantha said as she rode up. "He was doing well until that second. Maybe the wind scared him, or he thought he saw something."

Cindy groaned inwardly. Glory's neck was lathered with sweat, but he hadn't done that much running. He'd just worn himself out with nervous excitement. *Not a good sign,* Cindy thought.

"I didn't want to punish him," Samantha said. "He didn't act up to be mean—he was really going crazy. He must have some bad memories of the track."

"Probably he's remembering how he was treated when he was stolen." Ashleigh frowned.

Glory thrust his black muzzle over the fence into Cindy's hands, then jerked it away. He was still upset.

"It's too bad we don't know who Glory's trainer was," Ashleigh said. "If we did, it would save us a lot of guesswork. We could start piecing together what he learned, and subtract out what must have been done to him while he was stolen. But it's so hard to get any information from the estate of his former owner."

Cindy reached to rub Glory's nose. This time he permitted it. *Ashleigh must be disappointed in you,* she thought.

"Can you take him around again, Sammy?" Ashleigh asked. "Just a slow gallop for a mile, and then we'll quit with him for the day. I don't want to end on a bad note. And keep him away from the rail this time—he might go through it."

"Right." Samantha gathered the reins again and trotted Glory back out onto the track.

Whatever demon had tormented Glory during the first part of the work had evaporated, Cindy saw to her immense relief. This time Glory couldn't have been better. He followed all Samantha's signals, moving out easily into a canter and gallop. Cindy could tell from the spring in his strides that he was enjoying himself. When Samantha brought him back to the gap, he was barely winded. Cindy looked over at Ashleigh.

"That was fair," Ashleigh said as Samantha dismounted. "He doesn't seem green at all, really. Spooky, yes. It's going to be harder to wean him from those bad habits than it would have been to start him out right."

Samantha must have seen Cindy's expression, because she said quickly, "Shining was spooky too at first, remember? But look where she is now. We'll get him over that."

Cindy nodded. No doubt about it, her big sister had made Shining into a champion.

"Not bad!" Ian called to Cindy, walking up to the oval with Sagebrush.

Her dad must have seen the second part of the work, Cindy realized with relief. "Yeah, he looks pretty good," she said. Her voice was still a little shaky.

"Let's take Precocious out next," Ashleigh said to Samantha.

"Okay, I'll go get her," Samantha said.

"I'll cool out Glory." Cindy took the big gray's reins from Samantha. Glory rested his nose on her shoulder and huffed a little sigh.

Ashleigh smiled. "As soon as we get the kinks out of him, I want you to try riding him, Cindy," she said.

Cindy couldn't speak for a few seconds. Exercise riding Glory was her wildest dream come true! "But do you think I'm a good enough rider?" she finally managed to ask.

"Sure," Ashleigh said. "I started exercise riding Wonder when I was only a little older than you. I just have a feeling Glory will go well for you. He knows you the best and trusts you."

Cindy turned to Glory and hugged the big colt's silky neck. "Oh, Glory, that would be unbelievable. I know together we're going to burn up the track!"

THAT AFTERNOON CINDY, HEATHER, AND SAMANTHA DROVE over to the Nelsons' stable to help Tor with the Pony Commandos' lesson. In the big indoor ring, Tor already had cleared away most of the jumps he used with his advanced riders. He had set up four small jumps: two cross rails, evenly spaced, then a low, straight vertical, followed by a higher vertical. Three cavalletti, a stride apart, were in front of the other jumps.

"Cindy!" Mandy was waving at her from across the ring. She was already mounted on Butterball, the fat little candy-colored pony her parents had bought her last year. "I've got a surprise!"

"Come on over!" Cindy waved back.

Mandy headed her pony over to Cindy, posting to the trot.

Cindy's eyes widened. When had Mandy learned to do that? She wondered. Posting took a lot of balance and strength—especially for someone with leg braces. The other five disabled kids in the class, who were sitting on their ponies across the ring, applauded enthusiastically.

"What do you think of my surprise?" Mandy asked Cindy and Heather, her black eyes sparkling. "Tor promised to keep it a secret until I got it right. I've been coming early before class to practice for two weeks."

"You look like a pro, Mandy," Cindy said. Across the ring she saw Beth and Janet's astonished faces. Janet Roarsh was a physical therapist and Beth's partner in her aerobics business.

"That's absolutely fantastic," Heather agreed.

"I was tempted to tell about the surprise," Tor said, walking over from the jumps. "But I didn't."

"Very good!" Mandy nodded approvingly.

Tor grinned. "Take that pony around—do you think just because you can post, you deserve special treatment?" he teased.

Mandy laughed and trotted Butterball off to rejoin the other Commandos.

"That's an elegant jump course," Samantha said to Tor.

"It's simple, but I took some care with it. It's a real course—the rider has to get the horse's strides right to take the jumps correctly. Those verticals at the end are a stepping-stone to higher jumps. I actually designed it with Mandy's level of performance in mind," Tor admitted. "The others will benefit from it too, though. Okay, Commandos, warm up your ponies!" he called.

The six children in the group began to walk their ponies around the rail. They were assisted by Beth, Janet, Heather, and Cindy.

"That's fine, guys!" Tor called after the Commandos had walked and trotted their small mounts. "Now who's ready for a little jumping?"

"We are!" the kids called back loudly.

"Mandy first," Tor said.

"Why does she get to go first?" Charmaine Green asked, tossing her strawberry blond curls.

"So that the rest of you guys can watch what she does," Tor explained. "That's what you do in a jumping show—unless you're unlucky enough to be the first jumper in a class. You can learn how to take the course from the mistakes of the other riders."

"Thanks, Tor," Mandy said, laughing.

Cindy and Heather walked over and stood next to Tor. Because she was experienced in jumping, Samantha spotted the young riders over the jumps.

Mandy circled Butterball, preparing to jump. Cindy watched the younger girl take the cavallettis and lift over the first crossbar with ease and style.

"Mandy lets her pony jump," Tor commented to the rest of the class. "Heels down a little more, Mandy!" he yelled. "That's absolutely necessary for the horse to do its best, but it can't be learned," he went on. "Mandy knows instinctively how to make it easy for him."

"Her legs really are getting stronger, aren't they?" Cindy asked.

"Yes, they are," Tor said. "Beth and Janet have noticed that too. The doctors say if Mandy keeps improving at this rate, she may get her braces off in a year or so. They'll tell Mandy soon, when they're a little surer. But the amazing news is that the doctors are talking about a complete recovery now. Three years ago no one thought she would even walk again."

Cindy remembered Beth telling her that before Mandy started with the Pony Commandos, she had been depressed and angry. Mandy's parents had to coax and plead even to get her out of the house. Cindy watched Mandy expertly rein in Butterball after the last vertical and ride back to the end of the line, her face aglow. Cindy could hardly believe this was the same girl.

Tor coached the two other Commandos who were jumpers over the course. Cindy helped Beth and Samantha work with the three nonjumpers at a trot.

"Okay, guys—good work," Tor called. "See you next week."

"I can't wait!" said Aaron Fineberg, grinning as he rode over to join his parents at the side of the ring. A lot of the sadness had left Aaron's dark eyes since he'd become a Pony Commando.

Cindy, Heather, and Samantha collected the ponies while Beth and Janet helped the kids out of the ring to meet their parents. Cindy enjoyed listening to the animated discussions of the lesson that were going on.

"The Commandos really love coming here, don't they?" Heather asked as she walked Milk Dud over to the side of the ring.

"It makes them feel so good," Cindy said. "Beth says the kids enjoy the sense of freedom riding gives them. For once they can move as easily as anyone else."

Mandy walked quickly over, despite her heavy braces, leading Butterball. She took off her hard hat and tucked it under her arm.

"You looked super jumping, Mandy," Cindy said.

"Very professional," Heather added.

"Thanks!" Mandy gave them a huge smile.

"I'm going to take Sierra over a few jumps now," Samantha said to Tor. The big liver chestnut belonged to Whitebrook, but he was at the Nelsons' stable for the winter so that he could be jumped in the indoor ring. "Want to give me some pointers?" Samantha added.

"Will do," Tor said. "We've got to start getting him ready for the big Virginia 'chase in April." He turned to Heather. "Want to wait around, then I'll work with you for a little while?"

"Sure," Heather said shyly.

Cindy nudged Mandy. "Samantha's taking Sierra around. Show time," she whispered.

"Yeah," Mandy whispered back. "Let's watch."

Cindy, Heather, and Mandy clambered onto the low bleachers at the far end of the ring.

"Why is it show time?" Heather asked.

"I guess you've never seen Sierra worked. You're in for a treat." Cindy watched Samantha lead Sierra into the ring, say a few words to him, and mount up.

"Samantha's probably telling him to behave, but he never does," Cindy went on. "Sierra's workouts are a lot of fun to watch, partly because he's such a great steeplechaser, and partly because he's such a pain."

Mandy laughed. "Yeah, I've seen Samantha ride him before. Sierra never pulls the same trick twice."

"This ought to be good," Heather said. "Seeing Samantha jump Sierra might help me with my jumping."

Samantha rode the big horse around the ring, warming him up. Tor and a few of the older students set up a simple course of six jumps: a couple of easy cross rails first; then a three-foot vertical; two oxers, the last one three feet wide and fairly challenging; and finally a four-foot vertical.

"I don't want to push him, since we haven't been doing much with him, but that last vertical will make him work a little," Tor said. "Okay, Sierra, you monster. Let's see if you remember anything we taught you about jumping."

Samantha heeled Sierra into a collected canter and pointed him at the cross rails. Sierra lifted up dead center over the jumps and cantered smoothly toward the vertical and the oxers. He bounded over them as if they were cavalletti.

Cindy saw that Samantha's eyes were already on the last, highest vertical as she turned the big horse sharply to meet it.

"He can't fool around with a jump that high," Cindy commented. "He can't make up his mind at the last minute how to take it and then just pop it."

Sierra flew over the vertical perfectly, with room to spare.

"Excellent," Tor called.

"He's being a little too good," Samantha said. Before the last word was even out of her mouth, Sierra bucked. He came down hard on all fours and tried to grab the bit in his teeth.

Samantha gripped the reins tighter and didn't budge from the saddle. Cindy saw Sierra's neck arch as he strained against Samantha's hold, but he wasn't going anywhere.

"Nice try, Sierra, but you'll have to do better than that to get Samantha off," Mandy commented.

"He's just trying to intimidate me," Samantha called to Tor with a grin. "I think I'd be almost disappointed if he didn't try."

"Samantha's an incredible rider," Heather said.

"Someday I'm going to ride jumpers as well as she does," Mandy said emphatically.

"Someday I'm going to ride racehorses," Cindy said. A thrill raced along her spine when she remembered Ashleigh's promise. It wouldn't be long, Cindy thought, before she rode Glory on the track.

The next morning at school, Cindy looked proudly at her science project. Mr. Daniels, Cindy's sixth-grade teacher, had just given her an A on her work. The project looked back—four beady-eyed mice, twitching their pink noses and tails. Cindy had taught them to run through a complicated maze.

Max Smith sat to Cindy's left. Without really meaning to, Cindy glanced across at Max's desk. She saw that he'd gotten an A- on his project, a volcano that went off when he added certain chemicals.

Max started to cover up the grade with his hand, then shrugged. "You got an A by accident," he sneered.

"I always get good grades." Cindy sighed heavily. Max had started bugging her first thing this morning, when he made fun of the way she held her pencil. She was really getting sick of it. "Go find a lake and jump in it," she suggested halfheartedly.

"That's not even a joke." Max made a face.

"It wasn't meant to be," Cindy said, and wondered why she was bothering to have this conversation.

Max glared. The bell rang for lunch.

"What is his problem with me?" Cindy asked Heather. They'd grabbed their usual lunch table near the window. She and Heather usually sat by themselves. They were such close friends, Cindy really didn't care if she had any others. Heather was too shy to make friends easily.

"Whose problem?" Heather asked, peeling an orange.

"Don't pretend to be dumb," Cindy warned. She opened a can of apple juice. "Max Smith."

"I guess he's got a problem with you." Heather shrugged. "But he's so cute, a lot of the girls in our class wouldn't mind if he teased them. Like Sharon Rodgers."

"That's what you think." Cindy almost had to shout as another class spilled into the cafeteria, slamming trays onto the metal rungs of the lunch line and crackling paper bags.

Heather laughed. "There he is, over by the juice machine with Zack and Alex. Hey, Max is looking at you, and he *does* look mad."

Cindy refused to look back. "That's because I got an A on my science project and he only got an A-minus." Cindy unwrapped her sandwich and bit into it. Beth made great sandwiches. This one was tuna fish, but Beth had added dill to give it extra pizzazz.

"I got a B-plus on my project, which is good for me," Heather said. "Maybe Max is mad that you got a better grade because his mom's a vet. She might think he has to be a science star."

"So why does he have to take it out on me?" Cindy frowned. "Besides, he doesn't just hassle me about school stuff."

"I noticed." Heather popped a slice of orange into her mouth. "He talks to you all the time. I guess all you can do is ignore him. It would be pretty radical to tell Mr. Daniels."

"No, I wouldn't do that." Cindy sighed. "You're right—I just won't talk to him. Maybe then he'll forget about bothering me."

A crack of scarlet light was just creeping over the eastern hills when Cindy, Samantha, and Ashleigh parked in the stable yard at Townsend Acres Friday morning. They'd come to watch Townsend Princess's workout. Princess, Wonder's exquisite three-year-old daughter, was the only one of Wonder's offspring stabled at Townsend Acres. In the distance Cindy could see the dark shapes of the horses and exercise riders moving around the track, fading in and out of the early morning fog.

Cindy knew that Samantha and Ashleigh had horses to work and plenty of other things to do at Whitebrook, but they wanted to check on Princess. Princess looked perfectly sound now, but last year her racing career had almost ended. She had fractured a cannon bone in her foreleg when Lavinia, an inexperienced rider, tried to exercise ride her. Since then Ashleigh had kept a careful eye on Princess's progress. In less than a week the filly would leave for California to run in the prestigious Santa Anita Oaks race.

"Everybody be civil to the Townsends." Ashleigh grimaced as she got out of the car. "*All* the Townsends," she said, turning to look at Samantha. "Even Lavinia."

Samantha frowned. "I always wonder who told Lavinia she's the most superior person on earth."

"She can't even ride," Cindy said. "So Princess got hurt—"

"Lavinia's a jerk." Ashleigh ran a hand through her dark hair. "Let's try not to fight with her, though, guys. That just makes it worse to come over here. And I'm not going to abandon Princess, no matter what Lavinia does. At least I have strength in numbers these days—I remember when it was just me and Wonder against the Townsends. Lavinia wasn't here then, thank goodness."

"Speak of the devil," Samantha murmured as Lavinia crossed from the training barn to stand beside Ken Maddock, the head trainer at Townsend Acres. "What has she got on?"

"Knowing Lavinia, those boots with heels and the fawn trench coat are the latest style in barn wear," Ashleigh said, smiling a little.

"Yeah, right." Samantha rolled her eyes and followed Ashleigh to the training oval.

Cindy hung back at the car for another minute. She looked at the stream of magnificent gray, chestnut, black, and bay Thoroughbreds being led to the training oval for morning works; at the huge, beautifully kept training, breeding, and stallion barns; and at the Townsends' sumptuous stone manor house. Lavinia had so much, Cindy thought. Why was she always unhappy and determined to make other people unhappy?

Okay, so everybody says her mother neglected her when she was a kid, Cindy said to herself. *As if I haven't had it rough. I'd like to see how long Lavinia would have lasted in those foster homes I was in. She sure wouldn't have had fancy clothes. I had to wear hand-me-downs at least four other kids had worn first.*

That wasn't true anymore. Yesterday after school Beth had taken Cindy shopping for the California trip and to celebrate her excellent science grade. She'd gotten lots of great clothes. *It's hard to believe that a year ago no one would buy me a comic book,* Cindy thought as she joined Samantha and Ashleigh at the rail.

One of the regular Townsend Acres exercise riders was galloping Princess. Cindy's breath caught as the exquisite chestnut filly thundered by, breezing out the last quarter, her jockey crouched low over her neck. There was nothing like the sound of a Thoroughbred in high gear, racing like the wind, pounding down the track to the finish.

Ashleigh was intently studying Princess's movements.

"The quarter in twenty-three—very good." Ken Maddock looked over at Ashleigh and smiled. "She's up to form."

"No sign of the old problems?" Ashleigh asked tersely.

"Her leg's fine," Maddock said, obviously understanding Ashleigh's reference to Princess's injury. "We practically use a microscope to look at it every time she finishes a work. I haven't once found any heat or swelling."

"Good." Ashleigh nodded, but the tense expression didn't leave her face.

She'll always worry about Princess after she was hurt so badly, Cindy thought. Ken Maddock walked over to consult with one of the grooms, and Princess was led off the track. When she saw Ashleigh, she stopped and pricked her ears.

"Hey, beautiful," Ashleigh said, going over to stroke the mare's powerful shoulder. Princess swung her head around to gently lip Ashleigh's hand. "Hi, Johnny," Ashleigh added to Princess's exercise rider. Johnny Byard had ridden for Townsend Acres for several years.

"She's going really well," Johnny said reassuringly. "I don't feel any soreness or lameness."

Ashleigh cradled Princess's head in her arms. "I'll cool her out and bring her back if you want," Johnny offered.

"No, thanks—we really have to go. See you soon, girl," Ashleigh said softly.

Johnny dismounted and led Princess toward the barn. Ashleigh looked after them.

"It's hard to keep Princess here after this farm was responsible for breaking her leg, isn't it?" Samantha asked.

"Yes," Ashleigh said with a sigh. "But if I make waves about it, I'll just have to fight Mr. Townsend about training Mr. Wonderful at Whitebrook, since Mr. Townsend owns half of him too. I really, really want to keep Mr. Wonderful with us."

"When is Lavinia's baby due?" Samantha asked.

"End of May or early June. I know what you're thinking," Ashleigh said with a laugh. "When she has her baby, she'll be out of our hair for a while. But I think we'll be lucky if she's away from the barns for more than a day. I heard she's going to have a nanny to help out."

"Too bad." Samantha wrinkled her nose. "Cindy,

did Lavinia ever even thank you for saving her and the baby's lives?"

"Brad did. But she never mentioned it." A couple of months ago a runaway horse had knocked Lavinia down. If Cindy hadn't grabbed the horse and dragged him away, Lavinia would have been trampled. She'd almost lost the baby just from the fall.

Lavinia walked over to them. Samantha turned away, but Ashleigh put on a polite face. Cindy fought an impulse to run. Lavinia never missed an opportunity to say something belittling to her.

"Princess is coming along so well," Lavinia said, tucking a strand of blond hair under her rain scarf. "I think she'll blow away the field at Santa Anita."

Ashleigh frowned. Lavinia was famous for making remarks on training, about which she knew nothing.

"Oh, there goes Her Majesty," Lavinia said excitedly. Lavinia's bay mare was ridden onto the track for a work.

"She looks good," Ashleigh said with an effort.

"Her Majesty is in absolutely top form," Lavinia announced.

So is Shining, Cindy thought. Shining had beaten Her Majesty resoundingly in the horses' last two matchups. Something about the unpleasant expression that settled on Lavinia's face made Cindy think Lavinia was remembering too.

"What are you all doing here?" Lavinia asked. "Really, Ashleigh, you should get professional help with your horses. Schoolgirls just don't cut it."

"I'm a college student now. And Cindy is very knowledgeable about horses. Some people aren't, no matter how old they are," Samantha said coldly.

Lavinia stared at Samantha. "I don't see anyone asking you to run a racing stable, the way I do with my husband," she said. "This conversation is a waste of my time." She sauntered over to Ken Maddock. Samantha looked furious.

"Don't waste your breath," Ashleigh said with a sigh. "She's never going to learn or quit."

That's true, Cindy thought. *It's scary. I don't even want to think about what she'll do next.*

Cindy followed Beth off the plane at Los Angeles International Airport. The plane ride had been a blast. Beth had let her have the window seat, and Cindy had pressed her nose to the glass the entire flight. She had been thrilled to see the brown-and-green patchwork of Kentucky, the miles of almost black, freshly plowed farmland stretching across the Midwest, and the icy, glittering peaks of the Rockies.

"Let's grab a taxi to the track," Beth said, struggling through a large family reunion in front of the gate.

"I can't wait to see Shining," Cindy said excitedly. "I haven't seen her in weeks. Samantha said on the phone last night that Shining's putting in incredible works."

"I'll bet she misses you," Beth said. "Hang on to your suitcase, Cindy, or someone might walk off with it."

Outside the airport, Cindy blinked in the smoggy sunlight. The balmy air was very different from the chilly temperatures of early spring in Kentucky. The enormous waving fronds of the palm trees were also a switch from the soft, delicate green of the trees' first leaves back home.

Beth flagged a taxi and they rode to the track. Samantha, Ashleigh, Mr. McLean, and Mike were already there with Shining and the other Whitebrook horses racing the winter season at Santa Anita.

At the huge, prestigious Santa Anita track Beth and Cindy walked along what seemed to be miles of shedrows, looking for the Whitebrook stabling. "There's Samantha," Cindy said excitedly as she glimpsed the older girl's mane of red hair in front of one of the shed rows.

"You made it!" Samantha walked over and hugged them.

"And in one piece, I think," Beth said, kissing her. "Where's Ian?"

"He's out talking to another trainer. He said he'd be back in a few minutes."

Cindy saw Shining looking out of her stall. "Shining!" she cried, rushing over to hug the mare's neck. Shining bent her head and gently whoofed in Cindy's hair. "You look great!"

"She's ready for the race tomorrow," Mike said as he and Ashleigh walked out of the stall of Executive Decision, a three-year-old gelding that Whitebrook was racing at Santa Anita. "She did a half mile in forty-six seconds last week."

"I'm not asking for better than that even in the

race," Ashleigh said. "Right now we've got a little time off—why don't Samantha and I show you two around?" she asked Cindy and Beth.

"I'm kind of pooped," Beth admitted. "I think I'll just collapse in that director's chair by Shining's stall and wait for Ian."

"Beth and I will keep an eye on the horses," Mike promised.

Cindy walked with Ashleigh and Samantha through the track backside. Occasionally a horse whinnied sharply, but mostly the barn area was quiet. Almost all the horses were inside after the morning works, and the afternoon races wouldn't start for a couple of hours. Behind the track the San Gabriel Mountains shimmered hazy blue in the heat.

Most of the horses were looking out over their stall doors. A few laid back their ears when Cindy and Beth passed, but most of them stretched out eager necks, hoping for attention. Cindy patted a lot of soft gray, black, and brown noses.

They stopped at the Townsend Acres stabling to visit Princess. Ashleigh slipped inside the stall and ran her fingers through the mare's silky copper mane. Princess nudged Ashleigh affectionately.

"She's so much like Wonder," Ashleigh said as she let herself out of the stall. "And not just in looks. If she does well in her race on Sunday, we'll be pointing her toward the Derby in May."

"Wow," Cindy said. "Go for it, Princess!"

"You bet," Samantha agreed. "Should we go back

now and see if Dad's turned up yet? He'll want to see you, Cindy."

At the Whitebrook stabling Mike was reading on a folding chair outside Shining's stall. Ian and Beth were talking quietly together, holding hands.

After Cindy got a bear hug from her dad, Ian said, "How about we grab a bite at the track kitchen?"

"I'm there." Samantha grinned.

Cindy shook her head. "I'd rather stay with Shining."

"We'll bring you back a sandwich," Beth promised as the rest of the group set off.

"Great—thanks!" Cindy opened Shining's tack trunk to get out her brushes.

Shining whickered and pushed her chest against the stall door.

"Oh, I know. You poor thing—you've been so neglected," Cindy said. "I guess you want me to believe nobody's brushed you in a week."

Shining leaned over the door and looked eagerly at Cindy.

"Don't break that door," Cindy cautioned, grabbing a lead rope and letting Shining out. "The only stall left if you destroy this one might be in the Townsend Acres stabling. And you know what that means."

Shining shook out her mane.

"Yes," Cindy agreed. "You'd see Lavinia every day."

Cindy ran the dandy brush over Shining's glossy red-and-white coat. The mare sighed and half closed her eyes, clearly basking in the feel of the brush and the attention.

"Nice horse," someone said behind Cindy.

Cindy turned. An older man stood a few feet away, pushing back his hat. He was really looking Shining over.

Cindy figured he was a trainer. "Thank you," she said proudly.

"Your horse?" he asked.

"Kind of," Cindy said. "I'm her groom."

The man sat down on a hay bale. Cindy reminded herself to be careful. She wasn't sure what he wanted. She knew that sometimes before races other owners and trainers cased the backside, trying to get information to gauge the competition.

"Is she the only horse you groom?" he asked.

"No—I also groom March to Glory." Cindy loved being able to say it.

The man's face lit up. "That's a coincidence," he said. "Glory used to be my horse too, in a manner of speaking. I'm Ben Cavell. I trained him at Edgewood Farm in Virginia."

Cindy dropped her brush. "You did?" She couldn't believe what she was hearing. He could fill in all the missing pieces about Glory's past! "You're the person I want to see most in the world," she blurted.

Ben Cavell smiled. "And so are you," he said. "I've wondered a great deal about what happened to that horse. I did find out that Whitebrook bought him at the Keeneland auction in January."

"We just started training him—he's fast," Cindy said.

"He sure is," Ben agreed. "That was clear the first time I put him on a track."

"Can you tell me about his training?" Cindy asked eagerly, sitting on a hay bale near Shining. "Although I guess you should really tell Mike Reese and Ashleigh Griffen—they're Glory's owners."

"I think I'd rather talk to you." Ben's gray eyes appraised her. "Let's start at the beginning. I guess you know Just Victory is Glory's grandsire."

Cindy nodded. "And Just Victory is one of the greatest racehorses who ever lived. My dad told me that's good, but it doesn't mean Glory's going to be another Just Victory. Just Victory's colts and fillies aren't that fast."

"Not true," Ben said. "Just Victory sired a lot of stakes-winning horses. They're not Just Victorys, is all. Not every horse can win at a mile and a half by twenty-five lengths."

"Wow!" Cindy said. "I didn't know he won by that much. That's incredible."

"It is. So I've got a theory about Just Victory as a sire." Ben Cavell looked at Cindy thoughtfully. "Possibly whatever made him so special will never come out in one of his offspring. Or—and this is what I think—we're overdue for a colt or filly descended from him to be like him."

Cindy felt her face flush. "So you think Glory . . ."

"He disappeared before I was sure what I thought," Ben Cavell said. "I do know he was the most promising colt I ever trained. He's not just fast—a lot of horses are. He has presence, like his grandsire. He's built like Just Victory, too—Just Victory was a big horse, although he was black, not a gray. I was just about to race Glory for the first time when he was stolen."

At the far end of the barn Cindy saw Ashleigh, Mike, and Samantha approaching.

"I've got to get going," Ben said, rising. "It was nice talking to you."

"Wait," Cindy said, confused. "Don't you want to meet Mike and Ashleigh? Here they come."

Ben smiled. "I've already met them. Besides, you told me what I wanted to know—that Glory's in good hands. I know you'll make sure he gets his chance. A horse like him comes along once in a lifetime."

"But—" Cindy began.

"I'll talk to you all soon." Ben walked out a side door.

"Who was that?" Ashleigh called.

Cindy rushed up to her. "You're not going to believe it! That was Glory's first trainer—Ben Cavell."

Samantha and Ashleigh stared at her in astonishment. "*The* Ben Cavell?" Samantha asked. "He's one of the best trainers in the business!"

"He trained Bold News, a big stakes winner, last year," Ashleigh said excitedly. "This is fantastic, Cindy! I had no idea he was Glory's trainer. What did he say?"

"He said Glory's not just any horse—he may be the next Just Victory!" Cindy told them triumphantly.

Samantha laughed and shook her head. "Cindy, Ben Cavell knows a lot about horses, but the chances of that aren't very good. Every trainer is sure his unraced horse will be the next Just Victory! That's what's so thrilling about breeding and racing—until you run your horse, you could be right."

Cindy's face fell a little. "I suppose so," she said.

"Yes, but this is Ben Cavell talking," Ashleigh pointed out. "That gives his words some real weight. And Ben isn't free with words. He's really come into prominence as a trainer only in the past year or so, when his horses' records spoke for him."

"He must have taken a liking to you, Cindy, or he wouldn't have told you so much." Samantha smiled.

"I think he's taken a major liking to Glory," Cindy said. Samantha might have her doubts, but Cindy was sure Ben's predictions for Glory would come true.

SATURDAY WAS THE BIG DAY SHINING WOULD RACE IN THE Santa Anita Handicap. Just before the race Cindy rubbed a finishing cloth over the mare until her speckled red-and-white coat glittered.

She overheard Samantha and Ashleigh talking race strategy just outside the stall and leaned over the door to listen. Cindy wanted to understand how to train a successful racehorse so that she could help train Glory. Shining put her head over the door as if she wanted to hear too.

"We've drawn the number-three post position—that couldn't be better," Ashleigh said. "I'll try to take Shining right to the front and rate her just off the pacesetters. I'm a little worried about Destiny, the Irish horse. He's a speed horse, but he's got staying power too. Last month Destiny won the Donn Handicap by three lengths."

"That race was only a mile and an eighth, though," Samantha commented. "This one's a mile and a quarter."

"I know. Destiny might fade over the longer distance," Ashleigh said. "But I'm going to make sure I don't underestimate him."

"Right," Samantha said tightly. She looked over and saw Cindy. "Ready to take Shining to the receiving barn?" she asked.

"Yep," Cindy said, patting Shining's neck.

The big mare was ready to go. When Cindy opened the stall door, Shining lunged out and danced her hindquarters around at the end of the lead line.

"I'll change into my silks and meet you guys at the saddling paddock," Ashleigh said.

"Look how gorgeous Shining is," Cindy said admiringly as she and Samantha walked the mare to the receiving barn, where the track vet and track officials would check her over. The brilliant, hot afternoon sunshine turned Shining's flecked coat to burnished copper, and her black-and-white tail floated behind her like a banner. Anything could happen in horse racing, Cindy knew, but she was still sure Shining would win her race today.

Outside the saddling paddock Ashleigh mounted up and took the reins from Cindy. She looked professional and focused in the blue-and-white racing silks of Whitebrook.

"Good luck," Cindy said. She had noticed that Shining was going into the race as the clear favorite, at odds of 1.5 to 1.

"Thanks." Ashleigh gave Cindy and Samantha a thumbs-up and rode Shining onto the track.

"Ashleigh and I made a perfect game plan for the race, but the other jockeys aren't going to help us stick to it," Samantha said nervously as she and Cindy walked to their box seats. "Ashleigh will have to do a lot of improvising."

"She's good at that," Cindy said. She'd seen Ashleigh ride in several races and knew she was a top-notch jockey.

Cindy sat next to Mike in the grandstand and looked out to the track. The ten Thoroughbreds in the race had finished the post parade and were just beginning their warm-ups. Ashleigh had put Shining into a slow gallop.

Cindy tried to evaluate the competition one last time. Days of Chivalry, a powerfully built liver chestnut from Great Britain, looked good, but he was said to prefer running on turf. Indemnity had been racing well at the Gulfstream track in Florida over the winter, and the black horse might be a contender in this race. Destiny, the horse Ashleigh wanted to keep an eye on, looked composed and fit. The tall gray colt walked quietly out onto the track.

Her Majesty had been the last horse in the field to join the post parade. The classy bay had put in some good works at the track over the past couple of days. Cindy had seen Brad, Lavinia, and Mr. Townsend earlier, heading up to the clubhouse. Ashleigh had exchanged a few polite words with them.

Samantha looked out at the track and twisted her program. Beth squeezed Samantha's hand.

"Destiny's last two clockings at five eighths of a mile were better than Shining's," Samantha said nervously. "So were Her Majesty's."

"Stop psyching yourself out," Mike said. "You know Shining's in top form. We didn't want her to run any faster in her works and wear herself out."

"Besides, Shining has been in California for over a month. She's used to the weather and the track, and that gives her an edge." Ian leaned around Beth to smile encouragingly at Samantha.

"There goes Destiny," Beth remarked. "I didn't mean that negatively," she added with a laugh as the gray horse walked easily into the five gate position. The other horses loaded quickly too.

A second later the horses broke from the gate at the sound of the bell, a blur of speed and power. In the dust from the pounding hooves Cindy could hardly see Shining.

"It's Indemnity who establishes the early lead, by half a length," the announcer shouted. "Chivalry in second. But Shining is up close third, first time under the wire."

"Ashleigh and Destiny's jockey are rating them off the pacesetters," Samantha muttered. "We're going to have a late speed duel between those two."

"Solid fractions here. The opening half mile in forty-six and four fifths seconds," the announcer commented. The horses swept into the backstretch. Ashleigh hadn't yet made her move.

"Where's Her Majesty?" Cindy asked, scanning the field of rapidly moving horses.

"She's dead last. I don't think she's even going to be a contender." Samantha focused her binoculars.

Coming out of the far turn, Shining began to close relentlessly on Chivalry and Indemnity, going two wide. Clenching her fists, Cindy watched as Shining drew even with Chivalry and put him away. Then she shot up on Indemnity.

Destiny's jockey made his bid for the lead at almost the same moment. As the two tiring front-runners fell back, Destiny powered by them on the rail. He closed to within two lengths of Shining, then a length.

"I hope Ashleigh sees him in time," Cindy cried.

"She should. This is the race we were expecting," Samantha yelled over the excited cheers of the crowd.

Sure enough, Ashleigh glanced under her arm and kneaded her hands along Shining's neck, asking for speed. Shining had it!

The other jockey went for his whip at almost the same moment, but Cindy could see the gray colt would never catch Shining. Shining continued to draw clear of Destiny and the rest of the field, her long, fluid strides eating up the ground.

"Destiny is coming on hard. But this filly has speed to burn today! He's not going to catch her," the announcer shouted.

"Go, Shining!" Cindy screamed, jumping up and down. She was dimly aware that Samantha was pounding her shoulder.

Shining swept under the finish line. "She makes it look effortless," Ian said, clapping.

"She won by at least four lengths," Samantha cried, hugging Beth, her father, and a couple of strangers within reach. "I can hardly believe it!"

They fought through the crowd to the winner's circle. Her Majesty was just leaving the track. Cindy saw with shock that the bay mare was hobbling on three legs. The beautiful horse was obviously in a lot of pain. Hank, the Townsends' head groom, was leading her. None of the Townsends were in sight.

Cindy winced for Her Majesty's sake, but then a wide grin split her face. Ashleigh was leading Shining into the winner's circle!

"Thanks, Ashleigh!" Samantha was beaming.

"We'll thank Shining with some carrots later," Ashleigh said, laughing.

She and Samantha were glowing with pride as they took their places beside Shining in the winner's circle. The roan mare stood quietly, her ears pricked, seeming to pose for the horde of photographers, reporters, and TV crews jostling in front of her.

"Shining, you couldn't have been better," Cindy cried. The mare was sweating some in the heat, but the race didn't seem to have taken much out of her. When Shining saw Cindy, she put her head down to be scratched behind the ears.

"In just a minute, girl," Cindy said, backing away. "Then I'll give you a cool bath and help you deal with all those itchy spots. But you've got to get your picture taken now."

To Cindy's surprise, Ashleigh motioned to her. "Come on, Cindy," she said. "Get in the pictures."

"You belong here too," Samantha agreed.

Cindy happily walked to Shining's head. The mare butted her affectionately with her nose, almost knocking Cindy over.

Suddenly one of the TV cameras pointed right at Cindy.

I'm a celebrity, she thought, smiling broadly. *And this won't be my last time in the winner's circle. Pretty soon Glory will be here too. I just know it.*

That night Mike treated them all to dinner at a fancy seafood restaurant in L.A., not far from the track, to celebrate Shining's victory. Everybody at the table ordered a different appetizer, and Cindy tried each one. She had never eaten such wonderful, strange food before.

"This is great," Cindy said, loading her fork with another bite of something chewy her dad had ordered. She popped it into her mouth. "What is it?"

The others exchanged looks. "Should we tell her?" Mike asked with a grin.

"It's squid," Ian said. Everyone at the table watched Cindy's reaction.

Cindy stopped eating and gulped. The squid went down. She had a sudden picture of a slimy gray creature crawling across the bottom of the sea—and then sliding down her throat. "Yuck," she choked out, reaching for her glass of soda.

"Try this, Cindy." Mike handed over another plate of appetizers. "You'll probably like octopus too."

"Maybe Cindy's had enough new seafood." Samantha's eyes were sparkling. Cindy thought she had never seen her big sister so happy. Samantha had been walking on air ever since Shining crossed the finish line that afternoon. "Besides, you only eat things with ten legs, not eight, right?" Samantha added.

With a grimace Cindy shoved the plate of appetizer toward Ashleigh. Everyone laughed again.

Ashleigh didn't notice the plate. She was picking at her food and wore a pensive expression. Mike put his arm around Ashleigh's shoulders.

"Sorry." Ashleigh shook her head. "I'm not being much fun, am I? And it's such a great day for Shining and Samantha, and everybody at Whitebrook."

"You're worried about Princess and the race tomorrow," Cindy said. Ashleigh was always quiet and tense before her horses' races, but especially when Princess ran.

"Yes, I'm worried." Ashleigh sighed. "But I shouldn't be. Princess's injured leg hasn't been a problem since she went back into training. Worrying doesn't help anyway."

"Have some octopus," Mike offered again.

"Thanks, I will." Ashleigh speared a piece with her fork and popped it into her mouth. For the first time that evening she laughed as she met Cindy's horrified gaze.

The group sat for another hour at the table, replaying Shining's victory for the twentieth time and splurging on lavish desserts. Cindy noticed with relief that Ashleigh seemed to have shaken her gloom.

"Shining came out of this race so well, I don't see any reason why she shouldn't stay at Santa Anita for the Santa Barbara Handicap in April," Samantha said. "She's proved herself as a turf horse. Of course, the Breeders' Cup in November is at the back of my mind. That'll pretty much cap Shining's career—I probably won't race her as a five-year-old."

Cindy was silent for a moment. Nobody knew it yet, but she had big plans for Glory at the Breeders' Cup too. "Why wouldn't you race Shining next year?" Cindy asked.

"Oh, we'll definitely see how it goes." Samantha sipped her coffee. "But if Shining makes it through a successful racing season this year, without injury, I should weigh whether it's worth taking the risk for another year. Besides, it's better financially for the farm if she becomes a broodmare at her peak value as a racehorse."

"Speaking of peak value, a little bird told me that Her Majesty shouldn't have set foot on the track," Ashleigh said. "She had heat in one of her forelegs. But apparently Lavinia insisted that the horse run. They gave Her Majesty a walloping dose of steroids so that she wouldn't feel the pain in her leg and sent her out."

"That should be against the law." Samantha shook her head. "So is she ruined?"

Ashleigh shrugged. "Time will tell, but I wouldn't be surprised—she ran a long race on an injured leg. All I can say is at least Lavinia treats only her horses that way. Ken Maddock has sworn to me he doesn't let her interfere with the other Townsend Acres horses, after what happened with Princess."

"Good," Samantha said. "She'd better not."

"Her Majesty may have been finished before this race," Mike said. "Injury or no, she just didn't seem to have the will to win. Lavinia may have overtrained or overraced her. Even before this happened, I thought she was starting to fade."

"I'm starting to fade, too," Beth said. "Isn't it time to head back to the motel and rest for tomorrow?"

"We don't want to have bags under our eyes when they take our picture in the winner's circle with Princess, do we, Ashleigh?" Samantha grinned.

"Anything but that," Ashleigh agreed. For just a second a shadow crossed her face. Cindy wondered if Ashleigh was right to have her fears.

The next morning Ashleigh, Samantha, and Cindy headed over to the Townsend Acres stabling at the track for a last look at Princess before the Santa Anita Oaks race. The rising sun lit the mountaintops with a clear line of yellow fire against a luminous blue sky. It was a gorgeous day to be at the races. Cindy hoped it would be a good day for Princess too.

"Morning, everyone," said Hank, putting down his newspaper.

"Hi, Hank. How's Princess?" Ashleigh asked.

"I just fed her, but she's barely eating," Hank said. "That filly doesn't ever eat much on race day. And she knows that's what's coming."

Ashleigh quickly let herself into Princess's stall. She hugged the mare, pressing her cheek against Princess's satiny neck.

"Ashleigh tries not to play favorites with her racehorses, but Princess is her big love," Samantha murmured. "Princess is so much like Wonder—in looks, and the way she runs. She's even headed for the Kentucky Derby, just like her dam. That's why Princess's injury half kills Ashleigh every time she even thinks about it."

Cindy glanced around. She certainly didn't want to see Lavinia this morning, the person responsible for Princess's fragile health and Her Majesty's ruin. "No Townsends in sight," she whispered to Samantha.

"They're not all that interested in the prerace activities," Samantha said. "But you can bet if Princess wins, they'll be the first to push into the winner's circle. They always practically shove Ashleigh right out of the photos. She doesn't care about publicity all that much, except that it's good for Whitebrook."

"I know," Cindy said. Lavinia and Brad's behavior was pretty sickening.

"How's Her Majesty?" Samantha asked Hank.

Hank shook his head. "She completely broke down out there—tore half the ligaments in her left fore. She won't race again."

"I'm sorry to hear that." Samantha shook her head.

Ashleigh ran her hands slowly over Princess's legs. "I don't see anything wrong with her," she said at last.

"Do both her front legs feel the same?" Cindy asked.

"The injured one will never really be normal—it's got some bumps," Ashleigh said, standing and brushing off her jeans. "But it feels the way it should, considering."

"Makes sense." Cindy wanted to ask if Princess's injured leg was as strong as the other one, but the concern in Ashleigh's face stopped her.

Ashleigh turned to Princess and hugged the beautiful mare again, as if she never wanted to let her go. She whispered something to the horse. Princess seemed to listen, flicking her ears. With her soft muzzle she gently lipped Ashleigh's hair.

"Okay, let's head up to the stands," Ashleigh finally said. With one last look at Princess, Ashleigh squared her shoulders and led them out of the barn. As Princess's official co-trainer, Ashleigh wouldn't be riding the mare.

A short time later Cindy watched from her seat with the group from Whitebrook as an exercise rider ponied Princess and Jeff McCauley, Princess's regular jockey, out to the gate. Princess was prancing and fighting for rein. She refused to load in the gate, even when two gate attendants got behind her and pushed.

"She's wired," Samantha commented.

"For Princess that's not necessarily bad," Ashleigh said tersely. "She usually is wired before a race. We'll see. She's going to have to put out her best effort to beat this field—a couple of these horses are coming off major wins."

"I wonder if Princess knows that," Cindy said.

Ashleigh gave a small smile. "Maybe. She acts as if she does, doesn't she?"

With two gate attendants at her head and two pushing, Princess finally almost bolted into the number-five gate slot. Cindy could see Jeff McCauley patting Princess's neck, trying to soothe her.

"I hope he can get her to stop moving and standing straight before they break," Mike said.

Ashleigh nodded wordlessly.

At the bell Princess shot out of the gate and angled along the rail.

"Good break," Ashleigh said, half rising from her seat. "Now she's in the lead, where she wants to be. Princess hates to be rated, so I always want her right out front from the beginning. Otherwise she uses herself up fighting to take the lead."

Princess held on to the lead as the field pounded across the backstretch. A couple of the other horses were gaining rapidly on her, though. Princess didn't increase her speed.

"Is she tiring?" Cindy whispered to her dad.

"I don't know, sweetie. She could be—the field's set very fast fractions for the first half mile," Ian answered.

The horses whipped around the far turn. Princess wasn't increasing her lead, but she was holding on.

"Yes!" Samantha yelled. "Go, baby!"

In the backstretch After the Fact, a late closer, suddenly shot up outside of Princess. "After the Fact is coming in between horses," the announcer called. "But it's still Townsend Princess!"

Jeff McCauley glanced over at After the Fact. The bay mare was up on Princess's flank. She continued to pull almost even with Princess.

"She's going to catch Princess at the wire," Cindy cried.

"No, she won't!" Ashleigh threw her hands into the air. "Princess has more left!"

Princess dug deeper and slowly drew ahead. Cindy could hardly believe her eyes. Where had Princess found that extra speed?

Princess roared across the finish to win it by a nose. "Townsend Princess wins it! An amazing effort by an amazing filly," the announcer shouted.

She's Wonder's daughter, all right, Cindy thought, feeling dazed. Ashleigh's eyes were filled with tears of pride. Mr. Townsend waved at them happily from the Townsends' box. Brad and Lavinia, Cindy noticed, did not wave.

After Ashleigh had posed in the winner's circle with the Townsends and answered what seemed like a hundred questions from the press, Cindy, Ashleigh, and Samantha walked Princess to her stall. The backside seemed quiet after the reporters' shouts and the din of the crowd. A few horses went by with their grooms, clopping softly in the sand, and the gentle whir of a hot walker sounded in the stable yard.

Cindy could see that Princess was tired. The beautiful mare hung her head, and her step had none of its earlier spring. Ashleigh walked very close to her horse and kept a hand on Princess's shoulder.

"The race took a lot out of her," Ashleigh said with a sigh. "I'm certainly not going to try to run her again before the Blue Grass in April. Maybe McCauley should have tried to rate her in this race—she's beat. I don't know if a victory is worth this kind of effort."

"Princess wouldn't have run any other way, would she?" Cindy asked. "She always tries her absolute best."

Ashleigh smiled gratefully. "Yes," she said. "She always runs her heart out."

"GLORY, I'M BACK!" CINDY RUSHED DOWN THE AISLE ON Sunday night to the big gray's stall. "Oh, boy, I missed you so much!"

Glory stuck his head over the stall door and whinnied. All the other horses in the barn looked out over their doors too, curious what the ruckus was about.

"I know, you've been starved for carrots and attention," Cindy said to Glory with a laugh, pulling a carrot out of her back pocket. "But I promise I'll make it up to you."

Glory lipped up the carrot and nosed Cindy's shirt. He seemed to be saying, That first one was a start.

Imp jumped up on the stall door and arched his back. "At least you had company," Cindy said to Glory, stroking the cat. Imp purred loudly.

"We had a great trip," Cindy continued, tucking

Imp under her arm and letting herself into Glory's stall. "I won't tell you everything, because someday you'll be racing at Santa Anita and you'll see for yourself. But it was hard to be away from you."

Cindy ran her hands over Glory's smooth neck, then scratched him under the chin, just where he liked it. The colt's big dark eyes half closed with enjoyment.

"I'll come back to say good night. But first I have to help Dad and Vic take care of the stallions," Cindy finally said. Ashleigh, Mike, and Samantha were still at Santa Anita, and with everyone else away, Len, Vic, and her dad were still finishing up the evening chores.

Glory opened his eyes and gave her a firm nudge with his nose.

"I know—you deserve more petting since I was gone so long. I'll come back in just a little while," she promised. Glory snorted.

A loud chorus of whinnies greeted Cindy when she walked into the stallions' barn. The stallions' barn was the noisiest of all the barns, especially in the spring. She could distinguish all five of the Whitebrook stallions' voices—every one of them was calling out.

"You guys are happy that it's spring, aren't you?" Cindy asked, smiling. Jazzman, a coal black stallion who had raced fabulously for Mike, let fly with a hoof, hitting the barn wall with a resounding thud.

"Take it easy," Cindy warned. Although the stallions in this barn were retired from racing and used only for breeding these days, she still didn't want one of them to injure a leg.

Cindy went down the aisle to Wonder's Pride's stall. The big chestnut stallion was looking over the stall door and whickered an affectionate greeting. "I'm glad to see you too," Cindy told him. "How about if I put you in crossties for just a minute while I clean your stall?"

Cindy took a rope down from the hook and led Pride to the nearest crossties. The horse followed obediently, but Cindy was careful not to let down her guard for even a second. Stallions could be unpredictable and dangerous—even as nice a stallion as Pride.

I ought to know. Cindy grimaced, rubbing her left arm. Pride had broken it last summer when he had gotten loose and trampled her. Cindy had been inexperienced enough then to think she could stop the frightened stallion by standing in front of him.

"Guess what your aunt did," Cindy said to the big horse, pushing a nearby wheelbarrow to his stall. "She won her race, and showed so much heart! I guess you're not surprised."

Pride pawed the concrete aisle lightly with one hoof.

"You probably miss racing sometimes," Cindy said. Pride now spent his days peacefully frolicking in the pasture, and his first crop of foals was due this spring. Some of them had already been born.

"I wonder if they'll have the speed and heart that you and Wonder do," Cindy said, forking soiled straw into the wheelbarrow. Breeding was a tricky thing, she knew. Wonder had proved herself to be a blue hen—a mare who produced a high percentage of superior foals—but her talents might pass only from her, not through the male line.

"It's good to be home, isn't it?" Ian walked up to Pride's stall.

Cindy jerked out of her daydream. "Yeah," she said, smiling. "It really is." Cindy had lived at Whitebrook for less than a year, but she couldn't imagine living anywhere else now.

"What were you thinking about?" her dad asked.

"Pride's foals." Cindy leaned on her pitchfork and looked at Pride. He was starting to squirm from being tied up so long, and she hastily went back to cleaning his stall. "I was just wondering if they'll be as good as he is."

"There's no way to know until they get out on the track, which won't be for another two years, at least," Ian said, scrutinizing Pride. "We've had good luck with our stallions around here, though. Jazzman's already produced several stakes winners."

"I guess I was really wondering about Glory," Cindy said. "You know, because of what Ben Cavell said about his Just Victory blood. Glory could be incredibly fast, like his grandsire."

"That's a good example of how unpredictable breeding can be," Ian said. "So much of being a great racehorse is a gift—the random combination of the sire and dam's genes that sometimes gives the offspring natural talent and heart. Glory's definitely got some talent, but as you know, so far Just Victory's descendants haven't been legendary, the way he was. Some vital spark has been missing."

Until now, Cindy thought. *And soon Glory will prove it.*

The next morning Cindy tugged irritably at her school locker. She couldn't get it open—because Max Smith had planted his foot on it, holding it shut. Max was laughing.

"Why don't you give it a rest?" Cindy asked. Sometimes she wondered if he'd still be pulling stupid tricks on her in high school.

Max shrugged, but he moved his foot. "I heard Shining and Princess won at Santa Anita," he said.

"Of course they did," Cindy said proudly. For just a second she wondered how he knew the horses' names. But of course Shining and Princess were famous by now. "They win almost all their races," Cindy added.

"Oh, they probably just get lucky, like you do in science." Max flashed her a cocky smile.

"*You're* lucky I'm even talking to you," Cindy said, yanking open her locker to get her books now that she could.

She turned to go to class. Sharon Rodgers and Danielle Hart, two of her classmates, were standing across the hall, giggling as they listened to Max tease her.

Cindy's cheeks flamed. This was so embarrassing.

"If I'm so lucky that you're talking to me, I guess

you'd better keep it up, right?" Max asked, following her down the hall.

Cindy didn't answer. She just walked faster. So did he.

Max didn't let up all day. "See that cage?" he said later that morning before science class, pointing to where Cindy's white mice were kept. "There's room in it for you."

"Really brilliant, Max," Cindy said, rolling her eyes.

Heather made a sympathetic face from across the room.

Sharon turned in her seat just ahead of Max and frowned. Cindy remembered that Heather had said Sharon had a crush on Max and wished he'd pay attention to her.

Be my guest, Cindy thought. She ignored Max's comments for the rest of the afternoon, but it wasn't easy.

After class she and Heather ran for their bus. "Yes! Max Smith was just caged on another bus," Cindy said as she bounded up the steps of her own. "Free at last!"

"Max bothers you so much he's even starting to get on *my* nerves," Heather said as she and Cindy slid into a seat together. "He's kind of cute, but not when he acts like that."

"I guess I don't really care." Cindy frowned. "At least Max isn't around at home, when I'm with the horses—that's the important part of the day. As long as I only have to see him at school, I'll survive. He has to get tired of bugging me eventually. I don't know why he does it."

"Maybe he thinks your good grades will rub off on him. What did you get on that history quiz?" Heather asked. "I didn't do too well. I think my mother's going to kill me."

"I did all right." Cindy had gotten another A, but she didn't want to brag.

She gazed out the window as the bus rolled along through the countryside. The thick, new spring grass was such a brilliant green, it looked like it had been painted onto the landscape. The sun shone warmly on mares and young foals, together in the paddocks. The foals awkwardly gamboled across the grass, nipping each other and kicking up their heels.

"Do you want to go for a ride after I finish my chores?" Cindy asked Heather.

"I'll call you." Heather shook her head. "It depends on whether my mother remembers to ask about that history quiz. If she sees my grade, I'll be grounded for sure."

"Bummer," Cindy said.

As she walked up the drive from the bus, Cindy saw a truck she didn't recognize parked in the stable yard. That must be the new vet's truck. Len had said the vet would be out often to check on Blues King, who still had a badly inflamed leg.

It'll be fun to meet the new vet, Cindy thought, dashing upstairs to change clothes. She loved watching vets work. Dr. Aines, Whitebrook's old vet who just retired, had always let her hold the horses and put on bandages. Maybe the new vet would let her help too.

After she had changed, Cindy grabbed a banana off the bunch in the kitchen and flew out of the house to the training barn. Good, the truck was still parked in front of the training barn—the vet hadn't left yet.

Glory whinnied piercingly when he saw her, but for once Cindy didn't go to him right away.

Instead she stopped dead with shock, then rushed back out and leaned against the side of the barn, pressing her hands to her hot cheeks. She had to be seeing things—or Max Smith was in there!

Cindy peered back inside. Max was holding Blues King while a slender, dark-haired woman Cindy didn't know bent over the horse's leg. That must be the new vet. Ian and Gene Reese stood nearby, talking to her.

Cindy took a deep breath and marched determinedly toward Glory's stall. This was *her* barn—Max wasn't going to drive her out of it. She would just ignore him and stick to her normal routine.

Except that I'm going to tack up Glory faster than I ever have in my life and gallop him a couple of miles away, Cindy thought.

Max stared at her as she passed.

"What are you doing here?" Cindy blurted, forgetting her vow of silence.

"Helping my mom." Max looked uncomfortable for a second. "She's the new vet out here."

"Oh." Cindy remembered that Heather had said Max's mother was a vet, but the possibility that she was Whitebrook's new vet hadn't occurred to her. *Why did Dad and Mike have to pick her?* Cindy thought. *There are a million large-animal vets in this area.*

"Hi, Cindy," Dr. Smith said, not looking up from Blues King's foot. "I've heard a lot about you."

"You have?" Cindy asked in surprise.

Max blushed and looked away.

"Everything I heard was good." Dr. Smith carefully placed Blues King's foot back on the ground and straightened up. "His infection seems to be clearing, but I'd like to check him twice a week for a while," she told Cindy's father and Mr. Reese.

"Sounds like a good safety precaution," Ian agreed, taking Blues King's lead from Max.

Cindy's mouth dropped open. No—Max couldn't be coming out here twice a week. She hadn't done anything to deserve this.

"I don't want the infection to spread or we could be in real trouble with that leg," Mr. Reese added.

Max was wandering up the aisle, looking in at the horses. He headed for Glory's stall.

Cindy caught up with him. "Hey, Max—you don't need to come out to help your mom," she said, thinking quickly. "I can do it."

"I want to go on rounds with her. I'm going to be a vet," Max said.

"Me too." *Why did I tell him that?* she wondered.

"You'd better hope you're smart," Max said.

"Well, I'm the one who gets A's in science," Cindy shot back.

Max frowned and looked away.

I guess I'm being a jerk, Cindy thought. But he deserved it—when had he ever been nice to her? "Excuse me," she said. "I have horses to take care of." Cindy grabbed Glory's grooming equipment and quickly went into his stall.

She heard a series of clunks as Dr. Smith tossed her tools into her medical bag. "Maybe they're going, boy," she muttered to Glory.

The colt snorted nervously and backed away from the stall door.

"Beautiful gray," somebody said.

Startled, Cindy looked behind her. Dr. Smith and Max were peering into Glory's stall.

"He's in perfect health to race this spring. I just checked him over," Dr. Smith added.

"Thank you," Cindy said. The Smiths seemed to be everywhere. Now what would they do? she wondered. To her relief the two heads disappeared from over the stall door. Cindy peeked out to see where they'd gone. Good—her dad was walking them out of the barn.

"Max and Cindy go to school together," Cindy heard Dr. Smith say. "He's wanted to see Whitebrook for weeks."

That didn't fit with what she knew of Max. "Why would he want to come over here?" Cindy asked Glory softly. "Just to bug me, I'll bet."

The colt snorted and stamped his foot. Either Glory was worried the vet had come to give him a shot or something, or the Smiths were making him nervous too.

"Max is welcome to come over anytime," Mr. McLean said hospitably.

Cindy ground her teeth. How could her father do this to her? She had a feeling he wasn't finished, either.

"Max and Cindy could go for a ride sometime," Mr. McLean said, confirming Cindy's worst fears. "Cindy rides almost every day, and I know she'd be glad to take Max around."

"Max would love that," Dr. Smith said. "He's an accomplished rider, but his horse came up lame with an abscess last week. Wouldn't you like to come over here and ride, Max?"

Max mumbled a response.

Finally one of us got to say something, Cindy thought.

At last she heard the Smiths' truck start up. She was safe—but not for long.

"I think we'll be going on a lot of trail rides," Cindy told Glory. "But not with Max. We'll leave the minute I get home from school. That way, we can go by ourselves."

FOR THE NEXT TWO WEEKS MAX SHOWED UP AT WHITEBROOK every time his mother did. That was practically every day, since Blues King's leg infection wasn't responding well to the antibiotics Dr. Smith prescribed. Every time Ian asked Cindy if Max could ride with her, Cindy made sure she had plenty of excuses ready—she had homework to do, she'd twisted her ankle just a little, she had to clean her room.

"So how do you get Glory out for exercise without Max going with you?" Heather asked curiously during study period in the library one day.

"I ride in my school clothes so I don't have to change, and then I gallop Glory to the woods before the Smiths have time to drive over to the farm," Cindy said with a sigh. "I know—dumb, isn't it? But it's worked so far. And I'm not going to let Max keep me from riding Glory, because he really needs the work. His training's not going very well."

Mr. Daniels looked up from his table at the front of the room and frowned. Cindy bent over her history book and flipped a couple of pages.

"What's wrong with Glory's training?" Heather whispered as soon as Mr. Daniels had gone back to grading papers.

Cindy screwed up her face with worry. She tried to think how to explain exactly what was going on with Glory. This morning he had put in another unpredictable work—half good, half terrible. His works were almost always that way. In fact, that was the only predictable thing about them.

"One day he'll put in a decent performance long enough for his timings to be really good," Cindy whispered. "He obeys Samantha and puts his mind on business. At first Samantha and Ashleigh got all excited. They thought we'd finally turned him around, and he'd do that all the time."

Max Smith looked over from the table next to theirs and made an irritated face.

Cindy lowered her voice even more. "But then all of a sudden something scares Glory or he imagines something is going to hurt him, and he shies. Then unless Samantha really hangs on to him, he bolts."

Cindy dropped her chin into her hands. Sometimes when the imaginary terrors haunted him, Glory hung back and almost slouched around the oval, as if he wanted no part of being a racehorse. That was the worst of all.

She had written Ben Cavell at the Virginia farm

where Ashleigh said he now worked but had gotten no response. Probably at this time of year Ben was at different tracks with the horses he trained, she figured.

"What does Ashleigh think?" Heather whispered.

"Even she isn't sure what to make of it." Cindy shook her head.

"I can't study if they keep talking," Max announced loudly.

"Girls, if I have to speak to you again, I'm going to separate you," Mr. Daniels said sternly.

Cindy buried her nose in her book so that she wouldn't see Max's satisfied smirk. *He really is the biggest jerk of all time,* she thought.

Cindy was a little surprised that no one seemed to be planning anything for her twelfth birthday. March 29 was the very next day, and her family and Heather hadn't said a word about it. Cindy had dropped a few hints, but they hadn't seemed to get the message.

"Maybe birthdays aren't a big deal to my family or something," she told Glory that afternoon after school while she was picking his hooves. "I don't care that much about having a party or a cake. But just for once, I'd love for someone to give me a present. At all those foster homes I lived in, I never got one single thing."

Glory turned around and blew a soft, sweet breath on her hand.

"Yeah, I know, I get so much all year round," Cindy

said. She moved to Glory's other side and bent to pick up his foreleg. "But it looks like no one's even going to remember my birthday." She was surprised to feel tears form in her eyes.

Glory dropped his head to her eye level and whickered softly, as if he sympathized.

"Thanks, boy," Cindy said, setting Glory's foot down and rubbing her cheek against his. *Feeling sorry for myself never helps. I just have to face it—orphans, even adopted orphans, don't get birthday presents.*

The next morning Cindy bounded down the stairs. She'd told herself not to expect anything special for her birthday. But even so, she couldn't help looking around the kitchen for a package or other signs that a birthday celebration was in the works.

The kitchen looked the way it always did. So did her parents, who were drinking coffee and reading the paper. Samantha wasn't there—she was probably already at the barns.

"Well . . . good morning," Cindy said.

"Morning, sweetie," her dad answered pleasantly.

Cindy sat at the table and poured herself a bowl of cereal. *They really did forget,* she thought miserably. She tried to eat, but the cereal tasted like sawdust.

"Are we doing anything special today?" she asked.

"Not that I know of." Beth raised her eyebrows. "Is it a special day?"

"Um, no. Not really," Cindy said.

She dumped out her cereal in the sink and headed

for the training barn, kicking rocks on the path. *Why did I get my hopes up?* she thought. *I ought to know better by now. At least being around Glory will cheer me up.*

Cindy glanced in Glory's stall. "Morning, boy," she said, and started toward the feed room. Then she stopped short. "What on earth?" she muttered.

Cindy retraced her steps and looked in Glory's stall again. No, she hadn't imagined it. Glory was wearing a lei made of daisies around his neck. He was twisting his head and earnestly trying to bite it off.

What is going on? Cindy thought.

"Surprise!" Mike, Len, and Vic popped out of an empty stall next to Glory's. Beth walked into the barn, holding a huge white-frosted cake, which she set on the card table that Ian and Mike positioned in front of Glory's stall.

As Cindy stared in amazement, Samantha and Ashleigh jumped out of Mr. Wonderful's stall. Samantha carried a pile of brightly wrapped packages. Ashleigh was holding a small, flat package. The two older girls set the presents on the table.

"Happy birthday to you," Ian sang. The others joined in.

Cindy tried to smile, but she was still in shock.

"Open Ashleigh and Mike's present first," Samantha urged, handing Cindy the package Ashleigh had been carrying.

With trembling fingers, Cindy tore open the wrapping. Slowly she lifted out a blue-and-white saddlecloth. In satin white letters, both sides said MARCH TO GLORY. Cindy opened the small card that had been attached to the package and read:

To our newest exercise rider—you and Glory are on your way to the top! Love, Ashleigh and Mike.

Cindy burst into tears.

"Cindy, what's the matter?" Samantha asked with alarm. "Don't you like it?"

"It's just beautiful," Cindy managed to get out through her sobs. "That's why I'm crying. I've never gotten anything so wonderful before. I've never gotten anything at all. I didn't think . . . I thought you forgot. . . ."

"Oh, Cindy!" Beth put her arm around Cindy's shoulders. "When have we ever forgotten a birthday around here? And the celebration's just beginning. Heather's coming over tonight, and we'll eat this cake and have a real party with all the trimmings. You can open the rest of your presents now or later, whichever you want."

Cindy looked at the concerned, loving faces around her. *How could I be luckier?* she thought. *This is going to be the best birthday anyone ever had.*

"Glory, get out of there!" Ashleigh yelled. Cindy turned to see the gray colt lipping up a corner of the cake. Glory jumped back guiltily, but his muzzle was covered with incriminating white icing.

"It's okay, he can have some," Cindy said, laughing

through her tears. "It's his special day too. He makes every day special for me."

"All right," Ashleigh said the next morning as she gave Samantha a leg into Glory's saddle. "We've got to make some progress. Race day is in less than a month."

Cindy climbed up on the bottom rail of the fence and frowned worriedly. Last night she'd had a great party. Heather had come over, and Cindy's dad had blown up about a thousand balloons with her name on them. The group had celebrated with the sumptuous cake, ripple-fudge ice cream, and root beer. In addition to the saddlecloth for Glory, Cindy had gotten an expensive new bridle from England for him, complete with rainbow-colored, easy-to-grip rubber training reins. Heather's present was a video showing Secretariat, Seattle Slew, Just Victory, and other champions running in their races.

But now the party was over, and they had to get back to work. At some point, Cindy knew, Ashleigh would scratch Glory from his first race if he kept acting up. Otherwise, the risk of injury to him or other riders would be too great.

Cindy wondered how much longer Glory had to shape up. At least they'd had one pleasant surprise with him—yesterday they'd learned that Glory had no problem with breaking from the practice gate.

"So if he would just run . . . ," Cindy murmured.

Glory looked magnificent as always, and his step

was full of spring as he snorted in the crisp morning air. The big colt walked eagerly out onto the track. He looked ready to go.

Come on, Glory, Cindy willed him. *I hope you don't just look good today. Your whole future may be at stake here.*

Samantha tightened the reins and gave Cindy a reassuring smile. Cindy felt far from reassured, though. Glory had just wasted too much time these past few weeks.

Besides, there was something funny about the way he was moving all of a sudden . . . Cindy watched Glory closely. She didn't like what she saw. Under his gleaming gray coat the big colt's muscles were tense, almost twitching. The whites of his eyes showed as he looked nervously around.

"Glory, take it easy," Cindy called.

The horse flicked an ear in her direction. He walked on normally for a few steps, then his ears pricked sharply forward and he jumped sideways. Cindy wondered if she should warn Samantha that Glory was probably going to be a handful today.

"Cut it out," Samantha said, walking Glory over to the rail. "No funny business today."

Cindy relaxed a little when Glory tossed his head but obediently went into a warm-up trot and canter around the track. Not a sour note so far.

"Good," Ashleigh commented. "He's got beautiful movements, Cindy—when he puts his mind to it."

Cindy nodded. She knew, though, that Glory had to do more than canter nicely to win a race.

Samantha asked Glory for a slow gallop. The big colt bounded enthusiastically into the faster gait.

"Maybe we'll breeze him today," Ashleigh said, sounding hopeful.

Cindy was watching Glory uneasily. The colt had pricked his ears again. That wasn't good—he was focused on something besides his rider.

Suddenly Glory braced his legs and in three bone-rattling jerks skidded to a dead stop. Samantha was caught completely by surprise. She pitched forward, grabbed desperately for Glory's mane, and missed. She somersaulted over his head, hitting the track hard on her shoulder. Samantha rolled on her back and lay still.

"Sammy!" Cindy stared in horror at the motionless figure on the track. Her heart thumped crazily with fright.

"Wait here," Ashleigh said, already running toward the horse and rider.

But before Ashleigh could reach her, Samantha slowly sat up. "I'm okay," she called.

"Glory!" Cindy yelled angrily, striding across the track to him.

The big colt hadn't run away after he'd dumped Samantha. He stood right next to her, with his head lowered repentantly. Cindy was still mad at him—he could have killed Samantha!

"From a gallop to a dead stop in two seconds—that was a move worthy of a roping horse," Ashleigh said as she and Samantha walked back to the gap with Glory. "I never saw a Thoroughbred try that one, though."

"Are you really all right, Sammy?" Cindy asked as she took Glory's reins from Ashleigh. Samantha was rubbing her left shoulder.

"Just shook up. I told you how to fall, didn't I, Cindy?" Samantha said wryly. "In case I didn't or you forgot, always tuck your head, so that you don't break your neck, and try to take the impact of a flip like that on your shoulder. I think you're going to need to know how to fall when you ride this guy."

Cindy was surprised that anyone was even considering letting her ride Glory after his bad behavior today. The big colt gave her an exploratory nudge with his nose, seeming to wonder if he was forgiven.

"Glory, what gets into you?" Cindy asked, looking into his soft dark eyes. "It's spring, and there are a lot of funny noises, like birds twittering. Maybe even grass makes noise when it grows. I can't make spring go away just so you won't be scared of anything."

Samantha laughed. Glory put his head in Cindy's arms, seeming totally abashed.

"I know," Cindy said. "You didn't mean it. But that doesn't help, Glory."

Ashleigh gave Samantha a leg back into the saddle. "One more time," Ashleigh said. "Take him around again, Sammy. Use your judgment about what to do—if he's still flying off the handle, just canter."

Cindy was impressed that Samantha was getting back on Glory so soon, but she knew it was necessary. They couldn't end the work on such a bad note. And

Glory couldn't think that kind of behavior was rewarded by a romp in the paddock.

Cindy handed Samantha the reins and reluctantly stepped back. Although she knew it was strange, the more Glory acted up, the more Cindy wanted to ride him herself. She just couldn't believe that the sweet, affectionate horse who greeted her so joyously whenever he saw her and treated her so gently would ever hurt her. And even if he did, Glory was her responsibility. She'd convinced Ashleigh and Mike to buy him for Whitebrook.

"I'm really sorry Glory is being so awful, Sammy," Cindy said uncertainly.

"Don't worry about it." Samantha tossed back her red ponytail and flashed Cindy a smile. "It was partly my fault—he was going so well, I kind of dozed off. I should know better."

"No harm done," Ashleigh said.

"I see harm done," Cindy muttered. "Here it comes." Ian and Mike were walking in their direction. "I guess they saw the whole thing."

Somehow, by great good fortune, Ian and Mike had missed seeing Glory's worst shenanigans until this morning. That was probably because Samantha and Ashleigh worked Glory last, after Shining and all their other horses. By then Ian and Mike were usually inside doing office or stable work. The few times they had seen part of Glory's works, the gray colt had performed reasonably well.

Samantha eased Glory into a canter, then a slow

gallop. Cindy didn't want to take her eyes off Glory, but she couldn't help casting a distracted look at Mike and her father, who were fast approaching.

"Looks like you're running into real snags with Glory's training," Mike commented, leaning on the fence next to Ashleigh.

Cindy glanced at her dad. Ian was silent, watching Samantha. He was gripping the rail so hard his knuckles had turned white. Cindy knew he must be remembering how Samantha's mother had been killed when the horse she was riding threw her.

He must have been terrified when Samantha fell, Cindy thought, feeling bad for him. At the same time, though, she was worried that he would order Samantha to stop riding and yank Glory out of training.

"Glory's learning," Ashleigh said, keeping her eyes on the horse and rider. Samantha had the gray colt back into a smooth gallop, hugging the rail. Ashleigh turned briefly to Mike. "Come on, Mike. It's not that unusual for a rider to take a spill on a horse in training, even someone as accomplished as Samantha. It's not the end of the world."

"I've got to hand it to Glory," Mike said. "I thought Sammy could stick on any horse, even Sierra. Glory must really be something to top the antics of that evil-tempered animal."

Cindy closed her eyes. Mike was joking, but she didn't think this was funny.

"Sierra's thrown Samantha too," Ian said weakly.

"Look at Glory," Ashleigh interrupted.

Glory was running like the wind. Cindy could almost feel how cool the air would be at that pace and how swiftly Glory's hooves were eating up the ground with each powerful stride.

He acts like he's seeing angels now, she thought in wonder.

Glory pounded by the quarter pole. Ashleigh clicked on her stopwatch.

Mike and Ian stared at Glory. "He's going unbelievably fast," Mike said slowly. "Have you been breezing him in most of his works?"

"Not for the past couple." Ashleigh didn't take her eyes off the horse and rider.

Glory whipped by the mile marker post. Ashleigh clicked the stopwatch again. Samantha stood in her stirrups, signaling Glory to slow. The colt finally responded, shaking his mane and tugging on the reins.

Samantha pulled Glory up at the gap. Even before they stopped, Cindy could hear her praising him.

"Would anyone care to guess Glory's time for the quarter mile?" Ashleigh asked, waving the stopwatch.

"Fast," Mike said. "Very fast. Twenty-three?"

"Twenty-two and some." Ashleigh handed him the watch.

Mike whistled. "Holy cow! Maybe this guy's got a little Solidarity in him after all. Solidarity's early works were so fast, they blew everybody away."

Solidarity, Cindy knew, was Just Victory's sire and another of Glory's famous ancestors. She rushed over to the gray colt and hugged him. "Good going, boy!"

Glory snorted and tossed his head. He tolerated the hug for a moment, then pranced off a few paces. He seemed to know just how fine a performance he'd put in.

"Thanks, Sammy." Cindy looked up gratefully.

"Partly a PR job," Samantha said softly. "Glory seemed to be over his high jinks for today, and I thought he was up for a breeze. I knew Dad and Mike were watching."

"Great job, Sammy," Ashleigh called. She turned to Mike and Ian. "So after that run, do you think Glory's worth a little trouble?"

Ian sighed. "I guess I see your point, Ashleigh. I just wonder how much more trouble we're in for with him."

On the bus to school Cindy told Heather about Glory's strange, wonderful performance that morning. "I keep trying to think of how to get Glory to be more consistent," Cindy said. "It's like he gets out on the track and remembers his good training with Ben Cavell and does fine for a while. Then something sets him off, and he remembers when he was stolen and punished all the time. When he remembers the bad times, he flies off the handle."

"He's getting better, though, right?" Heather asked. "I mean, even Mike and your dad were impressed with him this morning."

"This is going to sound really conceited." Cindy frowned. "Glory's getting better for me, on the trails. But I don't think he's acting better for Samantha. He's still totally on again, off again. But maybe the difference is she's working him on the track," Cindy said quickly. "He seems to have really bad memories of that."

"Of course Glory goes better for you." Heather shrugged. "Why be afraid to say it? Glory's really your horse—he knows you and trusts you more than anyone else. It's kind of like I can talk to you, because we're friends, but I'm really shy around other people."

Cindy nodded and looked out the open window. The emerald grass was already thick in the fields, and spring flowers scented the air. She thought that she would love nothing more than to be out there at that moment, riding her beloved horse on the trails—or on the track.

But Ashleigh was the one who made the final decisions, and she hadn't mentioned the possibility of Cindy's exercise riding Glory again. Because of the way he acted for Samantha, Ashleigh probably thought he was still too dangerous for a novice rider. It was starting to look like Cindy would never get her chance to ride him on the track.

"We're running out of time before Glory's first race," Cindy said. "I'm getting awfully worried about that."

"You could skip that race and run him later in the season, couldn't you?" Heather asked.

"Yeah, but Glory's three. We already lost his two-year-old season when he was stolen. If he doesn't race soon . . ." Cindy dropped her chin on the seat in front of her. "It's really starting to look less and less likely that he'll run at all."

"He's too fast just to be a pleasure horse," Heather said. "Don't give up."

"I won't." Cindy was grateful for Heather's support, but Cindy still didn't have a clue how to improve Glory's track performances.

I wish Ben Cavell would show up and tell me what to do, she thought.

"LET'S TAKE GLORY AND SHINING OUT FOR A TRAIL RIDE," Samantha suggested Tuesday afternoon.

Cindy looked up from the peach she was eating in the kitchen for her after-school snack. "I'd love to!" Samantha always gave her riding pointers. "Do you really have time?"

"Today I do." Samantha reached into the fruit bowl to get a peach for herself. "Shining needs the exercise. She came out of her last race well, but I don't want to let her slack off." Shining had come in second in the El Ricon Handicap before returning home Sunday.

"I'd also like to watch Glory when someone else is riding him," Samantha went on. "That'll help me see what makes him tick. I've already got Shining tacked up in the barn."

"I'll have Glory ready in a second," Cindy said eagerly.

She tossed her peach pit in the trash and rushed to the training barn. Glory was hanging his handsome head over the stall door, clearly hoping for some action.

"I'm here, boy," Cindy said. "But today we're in a hurry. We don't want to keep Samantha waiting."

Glory wanted to have a little fun, though, before they left the barn. When Cindy tried to saddle him, he swung his hindquarters away. Cindy almost dropped the saddle, but she managed to throw it over Glory's back and cinch it.

"No more games," Cindy warned as she approached with the bridle.

But Glory wasn't through with her yet. He almost seemed to be laughing as he tossed his head first one way, then another to avoid the bit. Cindy finally got the bridle on by lassoing him with the headpiece.

"Spring is here, huh?" Cindy asked him as they walked out of the stable yard to meet Samantha and Shining on the lane. "You're feeling it. And look at Four Leaf Clover and Rainbow!" she said. The two yearlings were racing around the paddock, jostling each other and nipping each other's flanks.

Cindy felt a special fondness for Clover and Rainbow. They'd been her first roommates at Whitebrook. Samantha had found Cindy sleeping in the barn with the two orphan foals when she'd run away from a bad foster home. She and Len had bottle fed them.

"Those two are doing well," Samantha said. "You really helped bring them along."

"They helped me too," Cindy said. She couldn't imagine a better welcome to Whitebrook than taking care of the foals.

As she rode with Samantha into the woods, Cindy turned up her face under a halo of tender green leaves, relishing the smell of sun-warmed rain from yesterday's downpour and the busy rustling of animals. Glory didn't mind the changing sights and sounds at all. He danced through a puddle, seeming to enjoy the dramatic splash he made.

"I noticed you've been working Glory a lot on the trails lately," Samantha said. "It's definitely improving his works."

"He still acts up more than he should on the track." Cindy frowned.

"I think we can bring him around." Samantha reached up to touch the swollen buds on an oak twig.

"I do too," Cindy said. Right now she was sure of it. The dapple colt moved easily and confidently under her, his satiny coat hazy gray in the filtered sunlight.

Samantha was watching them. "You handle Glory well, Cindy," she said. "You've always had a natural seat and a good feel for a horse's mouth. You'll just get better the more you ride."

"Thanks." Cindy smiled.

"Have you been taking Glory out every day after school?" Samantha asked. "When I get back from classes, it seems like you two are always gone."

"I guess we do go out most days." Cindy's smile slipped a little when she remembered that Max Smith was the reason she had to rush out on the trails after school.

Cindy ran her fingers through Glory's thick black-and-gray mane and glanced at her big sister. Maybe Samantha could give her some advice on how to handle Max. "I've been trail riding partly to exercise Glory and partly to escape," she said.

"Escape what?" Samantha looked concerned.

"The new vet's son, Max Smith. He's a pain—in school he bugs me all the time, and now he keeps coming out to Whitebrook with his mother. Dr. Smith's been coming out practically every day to look at Blues King's leg. When I see her truck, I tack Glory up quick and ride into the woods."

Samantha laughed and shook her head. "I'm sorry, Cindy. I don't mean to take this lightly. It just sounds funny that you have to run away from home to avoid the Smiths. But Max really sounds like a pest."

"I don't know why he acts like that," Cindy said. "If he can't stand me, why doesn't he just ask the teacher to move him to the other side of the room? And why does he keep coming out here with his mother?"

"Maybe it's not what it seems," Samantha said cryptically. "You know what they say . . ."

"What?" Cindy was puzzled.

"That boys pay attention to girls they like."

"Fat chance," Cindy said firmly. *But what would I do if that was true?* she thought. *Then I'd have to figure out what I thought of him.*

Cindy woke the next morning in the predawn gray, staring at the grainy, indistinct black ceiling in her bedroom. "What a dream," she whispered.

She got up and looked outside. Day was just lightening the night, turning the deserted, misty fields black-gray.

Who was whipping Glory? Cindy thought, and shivered. In her dream Glory's tormenter had just been a huge, terrifying shape that descended out of the darkness. Glory had whinnied shrilly, desperately for help, and Cindy had tried to grab the whip. But Glory and the frightening shape kept moving just out of reach.

Suddenly Ben was there and seized the whip. He threw it away.

I'll help you, he had said. *I'll always be here, the way I was in the beginning.*

Cindy turned from the window to get dressed, shaking her head to clear it. "I wonder if that dream will come true?" she said aloud as she groped for jeans and a T-shirt.

No one was downstairs yet. Cindy quickly ate a bowl of cereal and let herself out the door. In the first daylight the barns were maroon with bluish trim, and heavy beads of moisture weighed down the grass. She could hear the stamps and cries of the horses in the barns, eager to be fed and put out in the paddocks. Cindy smiled as she recognized Glory's distinctive whinny.

Glory's work will go well today, Cindy thought. Or was that the voice from her dream?

Early as it was on Saturday, light gleamed from the barn windows. As Cindy hurried to the feed room to measure out Glory and Shining's grain, Ashleigh called to her from the office.

Cindy stuck her head around the door. "Hi," she said. "I thought I'd be the first here."

Ashleigh was punching numbers into a calculator and didn't look up. "Not by a long shot—I've been here for a couple of hours. Spring is a busy time, with breeding, foaling, and racing going on all at once. I want to talk to you about something. Just give me a sec to figure out these different feed proportions."

Cindy wondered what this could be about. Suddenly she felt afraid for Glory. Ashleigh was so busy. Maybe she'd run out of time to spend on him. She might have decided to scratch Glory from the race, take him out of training, and work with horses that had better prospects.

After a minute Ashleigh looked up. "Okay—that's done. Sorry to keep you waiting, Cindy. What I wanted to say is, why don't you work Glory this morning? Samantha's got four other horses to exercise, and she could use the help. Besides, I think he'll go well for you."

"Really?" Cindy felt her face flush with excitement. She couldn't believe what she was hearing.

"Really," Ashleigh reassured her. "Samantha said you looked great on him over the trails. He's a lot of horse, but we'll try it and see how it goes."

"Excellent," Cindy said happily. "Thanks!" She practically danced into Glory's stall.

Glory snorted and backed into a corner. He looked at her warily.

"You know something's up, don't you?" Cindy asked, reaching out a soothing hand. "But it's good, Glory—it's the best news ever! I'm your exercise rider now!"

Glory remained where he was for a moment, seeming to consider her words. Then he shook his mane and took a step toward her.

"I promise you it's okay," Cindy assured him.

Glory gave one last little snort, then stepped all the way over to her. Cindy quickly slipped on his halter and groomed him in the crossties.

"Mind your manners for Cindy," Len admonished Glory as he placed a light exercise saddle on the colt's back. The news that she was going to ride had spread fast.

"He will—I'm sure of it." Cindy couldn't stop smiling. She bridled Glory and led him out of the barn to the training oval. The gray was full of high spirits and pranced as far away from her as the reins allowed.

"You're in a great mood, aren't you?" she asked. "Let's see you turn that into a brilliant work."

Ashleigh gave Cindy a leg into the saddle. Then she looked at Glory for a moment. "Watch him," she said. "Don't let your attention wander just because he seems to be going well. You know what he's capable of."

"I'll be careful," Cindy promised.

"Good. Warm him up a couple of times around at a trot and a canter, then bring him back and we'll strategize."

Cindy squeezed her legs, signaling Glory to trot. The big horse tossed his head and moved out, his steps light and eager. Glory's hooves moved easily on the freshly harrowed surface, kicking up a light spray of dirt. His muscles bunched and released under his sleek coat.

Dawn had broken, and ribbons of red and orange clouds stretched across the sky. The rising sun lit Glory's coat in little shimmers of fire.

Cindy almost laughed. She stretched her arms over Glory's neck, savoring the feel of her beloved horse's quick, powerful strides beneath her. Glory easily changed gaits and direction, responsive to the slightest pressure of her legs or hands. Cindy closed her eyes briefly to bask in the moment.

When she opened them, she saw her dad watching them from the rail. *Oh, no!* she thought in horror. In the excitement, she had forgotten what he would think of her riding Glory. She was sure her dad remembered Samantha's recent fall.

Cindy resisted the impulse to gallop away at top speed before he could order her off Glory. *Dad won't want me to ride, not after what he's seen so far of Glory's works. I'm sure of that.*

Samantha rode over on Anmity, a two-year-old colt she was readying for summer races. "Don't worry, Cindy," she said. "Ashleigh already checked out with Dad whether you can ride Glory. He didn't like it at all, but he said he knew a lost cause when he saw one. I reminded him of the arguments he and I had years ago about whether I could work Fleet Goddess for Ashleigh. In the end, after Dad and I didn't speak to each other for a week, I was out on the track, on the horse."

Ian waved at Cindy, not very enthusiastically.

Cindy grinned and waved back.

"There are some advantages to being the youngest," Samantha said. "I blazed the trail for you."

"Thanks, Sammy," Cindy said gratefully.

"Okay, Cindy, canter Glory once around," Ashleigh called. "Keep him well in hand."

"Right." Cindy cued Glory to move into the faster gait. The big gray colt instantly responded, bounding into a canter almost from a standstill. He lengthened his strides and pulled on the reins.

Cindy could feel he was going to act up again—she might not be able to hold him! Cindy took a deep breath and forced herself to relax. "We're not going to run now," she said. "Soon, big guy. We have to do what Ashleigh wants and take it slow."

Glory responded, easing into a rhythmic, rocking canter. Even at the slow gait Glory's long strides swept them around the mile training oval in no time. Beaming, Cindy trotted Glory over to the gap to get further instructions from Ashleigh.

"Very nice." Ashleigh nodded. "Try him now at a slow gallop for three quarters of a mile."

As she headed Glory back out to the rail Cindy noticed that Mike, her dad, and Len had stopped what they were doing to watch her and Glory. She swallowed nervously. A lot depended on this work. It would be nice if Glory didn't decide now was the time to try a new trick—like one that pitched her into the dirt.

"But you wouldn't do that, would you?" she asked the colt, patting his neck as they cantered to the quarter pole. "We're a team. We'll show them."

Glory gave a quick, excited snort, as if he could hardly wait to. He powered out of the canter into a gallop. Cindy lost herself in the gray colt's magnificent action and the sweep of the chilly, fresh wind in her face. They flew by Anmity as if the other colt were standing still.

"Glory, I love you," she cried, her words blending with the thunder of his hooves as they swept around the first turn. "Oh, boy, this is so perfect!" She never wanted to stop.

But Ashleigh motioned them over as they galloped down the stretch. Reluctantly Cindy stood in the stirrups, asking Glory to slow. The entire Whitebrook stable staff was now lined up along the rail like a flock of birds to watch the work. As if he had noticed his audience too, Glory responded well to Cindy's commands, dropping into an easy canter, then a trot.

"That's enough for today," Ashleigh said when Cindy rode Glory over. "He hasn't been doing much until now. Good job, Cindy. He was really performing."

"I appreciate your letting me ride," Cindy said shyly.

"I didn't let you ride him out of charity." Ashleigh was looking closely at Glory. "I thought he might give his best for you. He's got a bond with you, kind of the way Wonder and I have."

You think we're in the same class as you and Wonder? Cindy stared at Ashleigh in astonishment. Out of the corner of her eye she saw her dad approaching.

"It's amazing what I've survived with you kids." Ian sighed. "But you and Glory did look great, honey, I have to admit. The colt's got talent."

Mike was looking at Glory quizzically. "I still don't quite believe what I just saw," he said.

"Believe it," Samantha said, trotting up on Anmity. "I think we're headed for race day with that guy, right, Ashleigh?"

"He's looking good," Ashleigh confirmed. "That light work didn't take a thing out of him. We'll step it up tomorrow with a longer gallop and maybe a quarter-mile breeze—if you don't misbehave," she added to Glory.

Cindy grinned. "Did you hear that, boy?"

Glory stood quietly, flicking back an ear as he listened to everyone talk about him. Cindy thought he looked quite pleased with himself.

Well, he's entitled to, she thought as she slid out of the colt's saddle and walked him to the barn. "That was wonderful, Glory," she told him. "You definitely deserve a big carrot, a long, good grooming, and a romp in the paddock." Glory rubbed his head on her arm, eating up her words.

"I'll cool him out for you," Len greeted her in the doorway. "I'm glad this big guy is finally behaving the way he's supposed to."

"Me too! Oh, Len, I know Glory's going places now!"

Glory pushed her with his nose and impatiently huffed out a breath.

"Sorry, boy," Cindy said, laughing. "I guess you're telling me that you know you're going to the Breeders' Cup next November, and a bunch of grade-one stakes races before that, but in the meantime you'd appreciate it if I got your tack off so you can go out in the paddock."

Glory snorted and pushed her harder, as if to say, That's *exactly* what I mean.

9

"HEY, YOU GUYS! WAIT!" MANDY JARVIS WAS RUNNING across the indoor ring at the Nelsons' stable that afternoon as fast as she could in her heavy leg braces.

Cindy stopped Milk Dud and Zorro, the two ponies she'd just finished grooming and tacking up for the Pony Commandos' class. Behind her were Samantha, Heather, and Tor, each leading a pony.

"Where's the fire?" Tor asked Mandy teasingly.

"No fire. Just listen to this. I'm getting my braces off in a year," Mandy said triumphantly. "The doctor said he's almost sure."

"Oh, Mandy! That's fantastic." Cindy hugged her.

"That's so wonderful, Mandy." Samantha had tears in her eyes. "That's the best news I've ever heard. Did you tell Beth and Janet?"

"I sure did," Mandy confirmed. "The minute I got here. They were blown away. So was I. You know this means I'll be riding on the Olympic team someday."

"I don't doubt it." Tor looked thoughtfully at the excited little girl and smiled.

"We should have a party to celebrate your good news," Heather said.

"Yep, we should. My parents are taking me to Disney World, too, in a couple of weeks." Mandy did a few clumsy skips.

"Did you tell the other kids in the class?" Samantha asked.

"I haven't yet, but I will right now," Mandy said. "They'll be so happy. Maybe they'll be the next ones to get better."

Cindy watched Mandy awkwardly run over to where Timmy sat with his mother. The small wheelchair-bound boy listened to her intently.

"Is Mandy going to make the other kids feel bad?" Samantha asked. "Beth said most of them aren't ever going to walk normally or even at all, short of a miracle."

"Well, Mandy's the one with the disability," Tor said. "Maybe she does know best what the other kids need to hear." He pointed at the Commandos and clapped. "Okay, kids, let's get this lesson rolling. I want everybody on the outside rail, warming up at a walk. Then we're going to trot some figure eights."

"No jumping?" Mandy called.

"Not today," Tor said. "We're going to work on control, suppleness, and balance. I know riding figure eights isn't glamorous, but without solid fundamentals your jumping won't be worth much."

For the next hour Tor coached the Commandos at riding figure eights at a walk, then a trot. Mandy and Aaron could post, and Tor showed them how to change diagonals at the midpoint of the eight, correctly following the movement of the horse's shoulder.

"That about wraps it up," Tor said. "Walk out your ponies."

"Can't we jump just a little?" Mandy insisted.

Tor winced. Cindy, who was helping Timmy stay in Milk Dud's saddle, was pretty sure she knew what Tor was thinking. Mandy wasn't tired, but most of the other riders in the class were. He didn't want to make the others feel bad because they couldn't keep up. At the same time, though, Tor wanted Mandy to learn as much as she could.

"Okay," Tor said at last. "Everybody else walk out their ponies. Sammy will watch you take just two jumps, Mandy."

Mandy clapped with glee as Tor set up a low cross rail and vertical for her in the center of the ring.

"Notice this is almost an in-and-out," Tor said. "You should take just two strides between the jumps. That means you'll have to collect Butterball right after the first jump and be prepared for the second. This is a little harder than anything you've done before. Are you sure you're not tired?"

Mandy shook her head. Cindy saw Mandy's father quietly enter the ring and stand against the wall. Cindy handed off Milk Dud to Beth and leaned against the wall next to Mr. Jarvis.

Mandy confidently gathered Butterball's reins and pointed him at the first jump. Cindy watched the little girl smoothly canter her pony toward the cross rail. Mandy's expression was intent.

"She's got almost perfect concentration," Tor murmured. "When she jumps, she's a hundred percent with the horse."

As Mandy flew over the jump, Cindy suddenly imagined her in a few years, with her braces off and taller, on a horse, not a plump little pony—and taking five-foot jumps.

"She's really got star quality," Cindy said to Heather, who had been helping Charmaine walk over to her parents.

"Yeah, even I can see that, and I just started jumping," Heather agreed.

Tor motioned Mandy over. She sat tall in the saddle, her eyes shining, as she posted on Butterball.

"I've been thinking, Mandy," Tor began. "I'm not sure you belong with the Pony Commandos anymore."

"I don't?" Mandy sounded stricken.

"You don't," Samantha confirmed, walking up behind her.

Mandy looked from one to the other. "But I thought you said I've been doing okay . . . ," she began, her voice trembling.

"That's just it. I think you're ready for some private lessons," Tor said. "I already spoke to your parents about it."

"Whoopee!" Mandy yelled. "Oh, Tor, you're the most fantastic, super guy . . ."

"Okay, okay, calm down." Tor laughed. "You've probably got the next ten years to thank me. Heather, why don't you bring out Sasha and I'll work a little with you now."

Mandy's tall, slender father walked over. "Good news, isn't it, sweetie?"

"The best," Mandy almost yelled, taking his arm and propelling him across the ring. Butterball walked placidly behind them. Mr. Jarvis looked back, exchanging proud glances with Samantha and Tor. They couldn't be happier that Mandy was one step closer to fulfilling her dream of jumping professionally, Cindy knew.

"I'll get Sasha," Heather said. Moments later she led out the bay filly she'd been riding for her jumping lessons. Sasha was a sweet-tempered, experienced jumper. Heather had paid close attention to what Tor and Samantha had told her about jumping so far, and she had made a lot of progress in her first few lessons.

Cindy settled back into the bleachers to watch her friend. Tor had Heather warm up, then ride over the same jumps Mandy had just taken.

Samantha sat down next to Cindy, propping her boots on the row of bleachers in front of them. "Heather's doing well," she commented.

"Yeah, she is," Cindy agreed.

Heather took the vertical without a hitch but bounced a little on the landing.

"Lean forward and go with him," Tor called.

It crossed Cindy's mind that despite Mandy's disability, Mandy was naturally better at jumping than Heather. Cindy felt a little guilty at seeming to prefer one of her friends over the other, but it was the truth.

"Heather's doing great, but I think Mandy really will ride with the Olympic team someday," Cindy said. She couldn't wait to see it happen.

Early the next morning, Cindy crouched low in the saddle, kneading her hands into Glory's neck. "Go, big guy!" she whispered. "Show them everything you've got."

In the dim light of dawn Glory shot along the rail, a gray torpedo in motion. The track was still damp with dew, and Glory's pounding hooves threw thick clods of earth behind them.

Samantha was just leading Shining from the track. Glory wasn't the last horse to be worked anymore.

The big gray powered along the stretch, his thick mane blowing into Cindy's face. The people at the rail were a blur. These days, almost everybody at Whitebrook turned out to watch Glory work. Even Mike thought he had real prospects.

Cindy felt Glory reach for more ground. She kneaded his neck again to encourage him, not to ask for more speed. She thought he was already giving the breeze his all.

But to her amazement, the big colt shifted gears again and roared down the track. They whipped past the mile post so fast, Cindy wasn't sure for a second which post it was.

Laughing in triumph, Cindy pulled Glory up and cantered him to the gap. "You're just amazing, boy!" she cried. Glory was skittering and prancing, as if they'd just gone for a short trail ride instead of thundering through a quarter-mile breeze.

Ashleigh and Mike stood at the rail. Ian was out on the track, talking to the exercise rider on Polar Danzig. Cindy knew her dad watched her work Glory for as long as he could stand, then did something else. He was still terrified she would get hurt.

Ashleigh tossed the stopwatch in the air and caught it. "I'm not complaining," she said. "The quarter in a shade over twenty-three."

"Glory's doing great," Mike agreed. "He was increasing his speed through the whole breeze."

Cindy smiled and patted Glory proudly. He yanked at the reins, as if to say, Let's go around again!

"Not today," Cindy told him, guiding the big colt to the gap. "You've done well enough for now. Everybody thinks so."

But as she started to ride off toward the barn Cindy heard Mike say, "Glory looks like a sprinter to me."

Cindy stopped Glory in his tracks. Sprinters could run only short races of six or seven furlongs. If Glory was just a sprinter, he would never be able to run in the biggest, most prestigious races, like the Santa Anita Handicap or the Breeders' Cup Classic. They were all over a mile.

"Why do you think Glory looks like a sprinter?" Ashleigh asked Mike. "He's got the bloodlines to have staying power. Just Victory certainly did."

Glory fidgeted, tossing his head in the direction of the barn.

"Just a minute, boy," Cindy murmured, stroking his neck. "I want to hear this. They're talking about you."

"Glory's such a big animal, and with those sudden bursts of speed, that just says sprinter to me." Mike shrugged. "But of course it's too soon to say—maybe he can sustain that speed over the distance. I didn't mean to be negative. Besides, being a good sprinter is perfectly respectable."

"Solidarity's foals—" Ashleigh began.

"Yeah, I know. He was a prepotent stallion. And he could go the classic distances, even when he had arthritis, a heart condition, and splints."

Mike and Ashleigh looked over at Cindy. "Don't mind me," Mike said. "I think Glory's got a great future, believe me."

"That's okay," Cindy said slowly. Maybe she just wasn't understanding Mike right, but what he was saying sounded good to her. So, Glory was fast over short distances—all they'd breezed him at so far, never more than three eighths of a mile—and his great-grandfather had enough heart to run and win races even when he was in a lot of pain.

Not bad news at all. And Glory was perfectly healthy.

"I'll cool him out for you," Vic offered, walking over to them.

"Thanks," Cindy said, handing over Glory's reins. She liked to care for the big colt herself, but Ashleigh was just riding Mr. Wonderful onto the track. Cindy hadn't seen him work much, because she was almost always finishing her stable chores and getting Glory ready to go out while Mr. Wonderful was on the track.

Exercise riders took out Sagebrush and Matchless, both two-year-olds, to work with Mr. Wonderful. The three young horses would be exercised together to accustom them to running in a pack.

Mr. Wonderful stopped in the gap and looked around. Ashleigh let him take his time and get used to his surroundings. Then the three riders moved the young horses out at a canter.

The exquisite Thoroughbreds moved effortlessly down the track, their hooves lifting lightly and necks arched, ready for the signal to run. All three showed beauty, grace, and fine breeding. Which would be champions? Cindy wondered.

Cindy breathed in deeply the crisp, invigorating morning air and sighed happily. She couldn't imagine anywhere she'd rather be. Here she was on a Thoroughbred training and breeding farm, about to watch three of the finest colts in Kentucky run their fastest.

The exercise riders galloped the horses side by side along the backstretch, then guided them into the training gate. The colts had worked from the gate before and walked in obediently. At Mike's signal the young horses shot forward.

Mr. Wonderful and Matchless leapt out ahead, powerfully churning up the track. Sagebrush lagged, struggling to find his stride.

Samantha walked up next to Cindy. "Look at Mr. Wonderful go!" she said excitedly. "He's set for his maiden in two weeks. Matchless will probably start in April or May too."

The two leaders swept around the turn into the homestretch. Mr. Wonderful was gaining. Although he was going at a pretty good clip, he was throwing up his head a little and acting more like he was out for a romp than a race, Cindy thought.

"He's not having any trouble staying ahead of Matchless, is he?" she asked Samantha.

"No, he's playing around. Ashleigh will put a stop to that."

As Cindy watched, Ashleigh waved her whip in front of the colt's eye to get his attention. Sagebrush had finally got his legs under him and was coming up inside of Mr. Wonderful.

Suddenly Sagebrush lugged out and bumped him. Cindy stifled a cry of alarm, praying Mr. Wonderful wouldn't fall. But the young horse quickly got his legs under him again and charged on. He crossed the finish a length ahead of his rivals.

"He's smart," Ashleigh called as she trotted Mr. Wonderful by the gap. "It's a good sign that he didn't panic when he was bumped. He's going to have to get used to that in races."

Cindy watched the magnificent colt trot lightly along the rail. His honey-colored coat flashed in the sun, and a brisk breeze lifted his flaxen mane. Cindy wondered with a stab of envy how Glory would have done if he'd raced as a two-year-old. Because he'd been stolen and shuttled around, he'd lost that chance. With it he'd lost his chance at prestigious races like the Kentucky Derby, which was open only to three-year-olds. Glory was three now and he hadn't even raced yet.

Where would Glory be if his life had been easier? Cindy smiled. Glory might be at Townsend Acres or some other famous stable, and he might be a Triple Crown champion, but he wouldn't be with her. Glory's troubles had given her the chance of a lifetime with him.

"Hey, Cindy, is it a school holiday?" Ian called.

Startled, Cindy looked at her watch and gasped. She had just fifteen minutes to change, eat breakfast, and run for the bus.

"Next weekend Princess races in the Blue Grass at Keeneland," Cindy told Heather as they sat together on the bus. "That's going to be her last prep before the Kentucky Derby in May." Cindy stopped to catch her breath and pushed her wet hair out of her eyes. She'd been so late, the bus had started to go without her. She'd had to chase it all the way down to the main road until the driver saw her in his rearview mirror and stopped. Rain had started to come down heavily when she left the house.

"Is Princess going in as the favorite?" Heather asked.

"I'm not sure. It's going to be a tough race—it's a mile and an eighth, against both colts and fillies. Princess hasn't raced against colts since last fall. But she beat them then. Wonder never had much trouble against colts, either."

"I wouldn't worry," Heather said. "Princess really is like Wonder, isn't she?"

"Everybody thinks so. Do you want to come to the race with us?" Cindy asked. "It should be incredibly exciting. I love watching Princess run."

"Are you kidding?" Heather asked in amazement. "Of course I want to come. Thanks for asking me!"

"I just hope the Townsends don't cause any more trouble between now and then," Cindy said. "Ashleigh really had to fight them to let Princess have the last month off, since she raced at Santa Anita. Brad and Lavinia kept saying Princess should race once more between now and then."

"Don't the Townsends always want to race and race their horses, just to make more money?" Heather wrinkled her nose.

"I guess." Cindy shrugged. "Or they just didn't think it would hurt her to run again right away. Princess *did* seem to come out of the last race perfectly. Her leg was fine, and she didn't lose any weight. But

Ashleigh wanted her to have a really good rest between races, just to be sure."

"Ashleigh won the battle with the Townsends," Heather said. "Princess *didn't* race again."

"Yeah, but now the Townsends are mad at her, and not just Lavinia and Brad. Ashleigh said even Mr. Townsend is kind of mad, because everyone's fighting again and he doesn't like it."

"Like Ashleigh *wants* to fight with them," Heather said sarcastically. "Right."

Cindy watched rivulets of rain cascade down the bus window, as if the sky were melting. "I just hope the weather clears and the track dries out by this weekend," she said. "Princess doesn't like to run in mud."

On Saturday morning, Cindy and Heather piled into the car with Ian and Beth to head over to the Keeneland track for the Blue Grass race. Cindy took a deep breath of the cool, clear air and smiled contentedly. The bright sun arced over the trees, promising a gorgeous spring day.

"What a day for the Whitebrook horses' return home to Kentucky tracks!" Beth said cheerfully.

"The track will still be muddy, though," Ian remarked.

Cindy bit her lip with excitement. *I hope that doesn't matter,* she thought. *But the way Princess has been training, she should walk away with her race.*

"How did Glory do this morning?" Heather asked.

"He put in another good work." Cindy almost laughed. It was the third good work this week. Glory had gone superbly, even though the track had been muddy and one day it actually rained. Ashleigh thought so too. She'd also complimented Cindy on her riding.

By now everyone had stopped talking about how unreliable Glory was. Now the talk was just about his upcoming race, at Keeneland next Saturday.

"Ashleigh will start riding him early next week, to get used to him for the race," Cindy said. She wondered briefly how Glory would perform for Ashleigh. Ashleigh was one of the top jockeys in the country, but Glory wouldn't know that. He certainly hadn't behaved very well for Samantha—or anyone else but Cindy since Whitebrook had bought him.

Cindy pushed the thought aside. Glory had to go well for Ashleigh. He wasn't afraid of the track or his bad memories anymore. Glory was a racehorse, and he had to accept different riders. He couldn't just run for one person, especially when that person was her—she was only twelve. She couldn't ride Glory in a race without at least an apprentice jockey's license, and the track officials weren't in the habit of giving those to twelve-year-olds.

"We'll root for Glory the whole way at his first race." Beth turned around to smile at Cindy. "That'll be your moment of glory—and his."

Cindy smiled back. She was sure Beth was right. And it wouldn't be the last moment of glory for the gray colt. Cindy was sure of that too, despite Mike's continued insistence that Glory looked like a sprinter to him.

But Mike was wrong. He'd never ridden Glory. The colt had more to give, Cindy knew.

Dozens of spectators, carrying big picnic baskets and happily calling to friends, already crowded the grounds of the beautiful old Keeneland track. Everyone seemed to be in a great mood and ready for a day at the races.

"Hey, everyone," Ashleigh greeted them at the Whitebrook stabling. Along the shed row Matchless and Polar Danzig were looking out of their stalls, ears pricked. They would run in maiden races today early on the card. Princess had been vanned over that morning and was in the Townsend Acres stabling.

"Is everything all set?" Ian asked.

"Almost." Ashleigh frowned. "I'm going over to the Townsend Acres shed row to see Princess. Who wants to go with me?"

"We'll all go," Mike said.

"I don't think you'd better, Mike." Ashleigh shook her head. "You have even less tolerance for the Townsends than I do. And I really have to be careful with them right now. I think we've all reached our boiling point again."

"I'd like it if for once they'd be careful with *you*." Mike grimaced. "But you're probably right. Just call if you need backup."

"Will do," Ashleigh said.

"We're coming, aren't we, Cindy?" Samantha asked with a wry smile. "We're kind of the official Whitebrook delegation to Townsend Acres."

Cindy nodded. She knew she had to get used to people like Lavinia, and not be afraid of them. But she couldn't exactly say she enjoyed the experience of talking to Lavinia.

"I've never met the Townsends," Heather said nervously as they walked in between the shed rows.

"You're in for a treat," Cindy said.

"A rare treat," Samantha added.

"Let's not anticipate anything," Ashleigh said. "The Townsends may not even be there."

"We can only hope." Samantha shook her head.

"The track's listed as muddy," Ashleigh said to Samantha as they walked into one of the barns. In front of a stall at the end Cindy recognized Princess's tack trunk and blankets in Townsend Acres's green-and-gold stable colors. "I wasn't too happy to hear that—I was hoping it would have dried out more by now. Princess will have to make an extra effort to drive through it."

"She can do it," Samantha said confidently.

"Yes, I think so." Ashleigh frowned. "Where is Princess, anyway?"

"She's out back," Cindy said.

Hank was leading the beautiful mare around behind the shed row, talking soothingly to her. Princess was dancing her hindquarters around at the end of the line, then stopping to rear a little.

"Princess is really wired," Heather whispered to Cindy.

"Yeah. She looks gorgeous that way, though. She's so spirited." Cindy smiled.

Suddenly Cindy's smile slipped and an icy flash of panic raced along her spine. *Princess isn't moving right!*

That couldn't be. Why hadn't anyone else seen it?

Cindy tried to move closer to the filly to get a better look, but Princess wasn't making it easy to watch her movements. She pawed the ground and jumped sideways.

"Stand back, Cindy," Hank said calmly. "You know Princess is real gentle, but she's not herself before a race."

Before Cindy could move away, someone stepped in front of her.

"Don't upset the horse," Lavinia said in a loud, snobby voice. "I'd think as a groom you would at least know not to crowd around a racehorse."

"But—" Cindy began.

"Don't talk to Cindy like that," Samantha snapped.

Princess eyed them, snorted, and skittered to the end of the lead line. The excited tone of the conversation was definitely upsetting her even more.

"You see?" Lavinia pointed. "I think it's time you left."

"I'm not finished looking at Princess," Ashleigh said. She sounded exasperated. "Why do we have to go through this every time I come over to look at my horse? I want to make sure she's completely fit, especially since we'll be running her on a muddy track today."

Good, Ashleigh's going to keep looking at Princess, Cindy thought with relief. *If there's anything wrong, she'll see it.*

Lavinia smiled. "Are you planning to scratch Princess because the track is muddy?" she asked.

"No. Is that what Townsend Acres wants?" Ashleigh asked testily.

Cindy knew that Lavinia probably did want to scratch Princess, although Mr. Townsend almost certainly didn't. Lavinia hated to see any of Ashleigh's horses win.

"Of course we want her to run," Lavinia replied, throwing up her hands. "But *you* never seem to. First you axed the plan to have her run again at Santa Anita. Now you're backing out of this race. It's always something."

"A broken leg isn't just *something,* Lavinia," Samantha said angrily.

"Her leg isn't broken now. Are we ever going to run this horse?" Lavinia asked unpleasantly. "Because if we're not, we might as well just put her down on the farm and breed her."

Ashleigh flushed. Despite all Ashleigh's efforts at self-control, Cindy could see that Lavinia was getting to her.

Hank put Princess in her stall. That was the end of her walk—it clearly wasn't doing her any good, now that Lavinia had showed up.

Cindy walked quietly over to Princess's stall and looked over the half door. Princess was standing square and seemed a little calmer. Maybe nothing was wrong.

"What are you doing?" Heather whispered, coming up behind her. "You're going to get yelled at again."

"I thought Princess was limping," Cindy whispered back.

"Oh, no!" Heather stared at her. "Do you think her leg is—"

"Get *away* from that stall!" Lavinia shrieked.

"I have to look at Princess," Cindy said, her voice shaking. Screaming adults really scared her, but she wasn't going to budge if there was the slightest chance that something was wrong with Princess. Cindy was thankful that Heather stayed with her, although Heather had turned ashen.

"Honestly, Ashleigh, if you have to bring little girls around the stable, can't you make them . . . *mind*?" Lavinia went on.

Before Ashleigh could reply, Mr. Townsend walked up. "Almost race time," he said to Ashleigh. "How's our Princess?"

"She seems fine," Ashleigh said with an effort. Cindy noticed that as usual, the minute Mr. Townsend came around Lavinia shut up and put on a sweet smile.

"I had the track vet look her over. He didn't find any problems." Mr. Townsend smiled. "This is almost like the old days with Wonder, isn't it?"

Ashleigh managed to smile back. "I hope so," she said. "We've got to get up to the stands now. See you in the winner's circle, Mr. Townsend."

Cindy opened her mouth to speak, but Ashleigh was already striding away. Cindy made a desperate face at Heather and hurried after Ashleigh.

"I'm so sick of that line," Ashleigh muttered to

Samantha. "I want Princess to run just as much as anyone else. But I'm afraid all this arguing is clouding my judgment, and next time they'll push me into running her. Brad and Lavinia wouldn't scratch a horse as long as it could lift a hoof."

Ashleigh suddenly stopped and gave Cindy a half smile. "I'm sorry about what Lavinia said to you."

"It's okay," Cindy said. "But I'm not sure Princess is. I think she may be favoring one of her front legs."

Ashleigh turned on her heel and immediately went back to Princess's stall.

Brad and several of the Townsends' fashionably dressed friends stood in front of Princess's stall with Lavinia and Mr. Townsend. They all looked over in surprise as Ashleigh's group approached.

Lavinia gave an exasperated sigh. "Here comes the groom contingent again! Now what?"

"I'm Princess's half-owner, not a groom," Ashleigh said tersely.

"I didn't mean *you,*" Lavinia said, tossing back her blond hair.

"I need to look at Princess again," Ashleigh said. "Bring her out, please, Hank."

"Leave the horse where she is," Brad ordered. "I just heard what you've been doing around here. Haven't you upset her enough?"

"Brad," Ashleigh said, very slowly, *"I am going to look at my horse!"*

"Bring her out, Hank," Mr. Townsend said with a sigh.

Without a word, Hank led Princess out of the stall.

Brad was right that Princess was even more upset, Cindy thought unhappily. After all the fighting, Princess was a bundle of nerves. Hank could barely hold the mare as she yanked on the lead line, half rearing, and plunged across the stable aisle.

"What do you think is wrong, Ashleigh?" Mr. Townsend asked.

"I don't know. Cindy thought she was favoring one of her forelegs." Ashleigh ran her hands over Princess's legs, but it was difficult to do when Princess was skittering around so much. Hank led Princess up and down the aisle.

"I don't see anything," Ashleigh said at last. "Do you, Cindy?"

Cindy shook her head miserably. She couldn't point to anything wrong with the horse. But she still had a vague feeling that something about Princess's movements just wasn't right.

"We'd really better clear out and let Princess unwind," Ashleigh said reluctantly. "Thanks, Hank. Sorry, Mr. Townsend."

"It's all right," he said. "Better to be safe than sorry, especially with this horse."

"Do you think Princess is okay?" Heather asked Cindy softly as they walked back to the Whitebrook stabling.

Cindy wrinkled her forehead and shook her head. "No," she said. "But I don't know why, and you can't scratch a horse from a race just because you've got a feeling about something. I've got to have something definite."

"I guess you did everything you could," Heather said consolingly.

Cindy nodded. She couldn't think what else she could do either. But the prerace festivities were spoiled for her. She couldn't enjoy the gourmet picnic Beth had fixed, or relax on the blanket with her family, soaking in the rays of the strong noon sun, or enjoy the sight of the colorfully blanketed horses walking around the barns with their grooms.

"It's almost time for the first race," Ashleigh said, getting up and brushing off crumbs. She hadn't eaten much.

I hope I didn't make her worry more about Princess than she always does, Cindy thought as she followed her parents to the grandstand. *If there's nothing to worry about.*

Cindy sat on the edge of her seat in the grandstand as several of the smaller races went off before the Blue Grass. Matchless won his race, and Polar Danzig finished a strong second after being blocked. Mike and Ian were smiling broadly, but Cindy was too nervous about Princess to enjoy the good news much. She tried to take comfort in the fact that there hadn't been one track mishap so far.

Then the horses walked out onto the track for the Blue Grass post parade. Cindy spotted Princess next to an escort rider, with Jeff McCauley in the saddle, wearing Townsend Acres's green-and-gold silks.

Cindy focused her binoculars and desperately tried to see if Princess was moving wrong.

"How does she look?" Heather asked worriedly.

"I don't know. All those other horses keep getting in the way."

Cindy knew this was her last chance to stop Princess from racing. If Princess ran on an injured leg, she might die.

"I can see her, but I just can't tell if her movements are normal or not," Cindy said in frustration. "She's jumping around because she's so excited. Now I know what I should have done when we were over at the stall—I should have asked somebody to trot Princess until she was moving smoothly. That's what Dr. Smith did with Blues King."

"Too late now." Heather looked tense too.

The horses approached the gate. Princess had drawn a bad post position—ten, way on the outside.

"She'll have to break clean and get right out in front," Ashleigh said to Samantha. "That's her usual way of running, but if she misses her chance at the gate, she may not get another one."

"I'll bet she gets out clean," Samantha replied.

One of the horses refused to load into the gate. Cindy thought she might scream from the tension—she just wanted the race to be over. At last, with three gate attendants pulling and shoving, the last horse went in.

There was a moment of near silence. Then the gate flipped open and the bell clanged. "They're off!" the announcer shouted.

The ten Thoroughbreds in the race charged out of the gate, fighting for position. Jeff McCauley angled Princess across the track, trying to get her along the rail, but he only succeeded in cutting across part of the field.

"She's blocked," Ashleigh shouted as the horses thundered across the finish for the first time. "Just what I expected, with that post position."

"Jeff will find an opening," Mike said.

But as the horses poured into the backstretch, Princess still had nowhere to go. As everyone else around her tensed, Cindy relaxed. Although Princess was on the far side of the racetrack, a long ways off, she seemed to be running normally.

"Usually it's hard to see the horses on the backstretch, but I can see Princess perfectly this time," Ashleigh said, groaning. "She's behind a wall of six horses. We'll just have to hope some of them drop back soon."

"McCauley's trying to rate her, because she's trapped," Samantha said. "But she's fighting him!"

Suddenly Princess roared around the horses blocking her.

"And Townsend Princess is sent six wide," the announcer cried. "She's five lengths from the lead but gaining with every stride. And it's Townsend Princess who blazes the way around the far turn!"

Cindy watched Princess through her binoculars. Princess's copper-colored mane whipped back in the wind as she dug in.

"And Townsend Princess comes flying! A huge upset looming here. . . ."

Princess changed leads in the stretch to power for the finish. The beautiful mare reached for more ground with every stride, leaving the rest of the field in the mud.

Something's wrong! Cindy tried to focus her binoculars more clearly. Now she was positive. Princess was favoring her right fore, the leg she had broken! But she wasn't stopping, even though her pain must have been excruciating.

Frantic, Cindy dropped the binoculars and looked at Samantha and Ashleigh, trying to think what to say or do. Neither of them seemed to notice that anything was wrong.

Then Ashleigh put her hands to her mouth and gasped.

"You're killing her!" Cindy screamed. She hardly recognized her own voice. Her dad and Samantha gave her startled looks, but the roar of the crowd almost drowned out her words.

Cindy stared back out at the track. Now she didn't need her binoculars, because the horses were running for the wire, almost directly in front of her. Princess was falling apart! Her stride was jagged and labored. As Cindy watched, Princess bumped the horse next to her.

It's too late to do anything, Cindy realized. Princess reeled and almost crashed into the outside rail.

"Townsend Princess has broken down," the announcer's voice blared.

"No!" Ashleigh screamed. *"Princess!"*

By now McCauley was frantically trying to pull Princess up. Princess fought the restraint, shaking her head and attempting awkwardly to gallop after the other horses.

Desert Fury, the last horse in the field, shot by. As if she couldn't bear it, Princess gave one last game effort to pursue him, but she had only three legs to run on. She fell hard on her knees. McCauley went off over her head.

The Whitebrook group had frozen in horror. Track attendants and the track vet rushed out to Princess.

The rest of the horses charged across the finish line, but Cindy hardly noticed. She pushed out of the grandstand and ran after Ashleigh onto the track.

Princess was in agony. The beautiful mare had struggled back to her feet and held her right fore off the ground. Dirt from the track marred her copper coat. The whites of her frightened eyes showed as she fought off the vet and McCauley, rearing and yanking her head away. The men were trying desperately to restrain her.

"I've got to get near enough to tranquilize her," the vet said. "We have to get her to the clinic right away. If she puts weight on that leg, she could rip every last muscle and nerve in it. . . ."

Oh, no! Cindy thought in terror. *Will Princess lose her leg?*

"Princess, it's okay," Ashleigh said softly. She moved to the mare's side, seemingly unafraid of the panicking, rearing horse's slicing hooves.

Princess suddenly realized Ashleigh was there. She stopped rearing and whickered pathetically, putting her head down to Ashleigh's arms. She seemed to believe that the one person who could help her had come.

"It's okay, sweetie," Ashleigh soothed, stroking the horse's lathered neck. "We'll make it better." Ashleigh nodded at the vet.

Shuddering, Princess permitted the vet to give her the shot. Ashleigh stood at Princess's head while the tranquilizer took effect and the mare's pain receded. Cindy closed her eyes in relief.

The vet, McCauley, and several track attendants slowly loaded the drugged horse into an ambulance. "We'll meet you over at the clinic," the vet called. Ashleigh just nodded.

"I'm sorry, Ashleigh," McCauley said. His voice shook. He was so coated with mud, it was impossible to tell his silks had once been green and gold. "I just couldn't pull her up. . . . I tried."

"I know you did." Ashleigh seemed to be struggling for breath. "Nobody could ever stop her."

"Come on, Cindy," Ian said gently. "We'll go over to the clinic and get the word on Princess."

Cindy looked around. Her dad, Beth, Samantha, Heather, and Mike were standing behind Ashleigh. Their faces wore expressions of shock and sadness.

Mike laid a comforting arm on Ashleigh's shoulders, but she shook her head and walked off a few paces.

Cindy felt stunned. This was like a nightmare. She saw again how Princess thundered around the far turn, the way she threw up her head as she changed leads, on her way to victory . . . and fell, her leg broken, her career and possibly her life over.

This wasn't a nightmare. It was much worse, because it was real.

"Princess will never race again," Samantha said hollowly.

"No. She may have to be put down," Mike said quietly. "I'd say there's a good chance of that."

How could something so terrible happen so fast? Cindy wondered.

Ashleigh stood alone on the track where Princess had fallen, her face in her hands. Cindy tried to think what she could say to comfort Ashleigh, but there didn't seem to be anything.

"LAVINIA CAN DO WHATEVER SHE WANTS, RIGHT?" CINDY muttered as she stomped down the barn aisle before school the next day, pushing a big broom in front of her. "She's got so much money." Cindy furiously shook the broom out the back door of the barn and marched back down the other way.

She'd been sweeping the barn for about an hour now, trying to let out in physical activity some of her anger about what had happened to Princess. So far, it wasn't working. But the barn looked great.

Glory was leaning as far over his stall door as he could reach, watching her. He seemed to be trying to figure out what she was doing.

"Right, boy?" Cindy asked, sweeping the broom over to him. "Lavinia can destroy Princess's life and break Ashleigh's heart, but so what? Lavinia can just buy another horse with all her money and break its leg too. She ruined Her Majesty at Santa Anita, why not ruin Ashleigh's horse too?"

The night before, Cindy, Samantha, Ian, and Beth had returned to Whitebrook, just hours after the race that had ended Princess's racing career. Ashleigh, Mike, and Mr. Townsend were staying with Princess in Lexington, at the veterinary clinic.

Ashleigh had called Ian earlier this morning and said that so far the long, complicated operation on Princess was a success. The real question was whether Princess would tolerate the cast, the heavy bandages that encased her leg from hoof to shoulder, and the pain in her leg. She'd come through her first leg break, but this one was much worse.

"Boy, do I hate Lavinia." Cindy pushed her broom past the stalls of the other horses in the training barn, patting inquisitive noses as she went. "At least I got up the nerve to say I thought something was wrong with Princess before the race, in spite of that witch."

Princess would never run again, though. That much was dead certain.

Cindy gave the broom a violent push. Someone stuck out a foot and stopped it.

"What on earth are you doing?" Ashleigh asked. "The barn's spotless."

"You're back!" Cindy cried. "How's Princess?"

"We don't really know." Ashleigh looked exhausted from the strain and lack of sleep. "The radiographs showed that Princess actually broke two bones—her right-front cannon, which is what she broke before, and the lateral sesamoid in the same leg. The vets inserted screws to stabilize the fractures. We won't know for a while if Princess will tolerate the injuries. If she goes crazy and rips off the cast, we'll have to put her down."

Cindy swallowed. Tears sprang to her eyes.

"I'm sorry, Cindy." Ashleigh sounded contrite. "I don't mean to put everything so negatively. I'm just so tired and sad."

"I know." Cindy hesitated. "I'm really sorry I didn't know how to say what was wrong with Princess before the race. Maybe if I had, you wouldn't have raced her."

"You did everything you could," Ashleigh said gently. "I didn't see anything wrong, and neither did the track vet when he checked her before the race. Either nothing *was* wrong, and Princess's leg broke again just because she stressed it particularly hard at that point in the race, or you saw something wrong that was so subtle the rest of us missed it. I think you probably did see something—your eyes must be better than the rest of ours. You might think about being a vet someday."

Cindy smiled a little at the praise. "I am," she said.

"Good. Anyway, the point is this would have happened to Princess sooner or later, given her history of injury," Ashleigh said wearily. "We just have to deal with it."

Cindy looked at the broom. "I'll try," she said.

"Hey, the news isn't all bad." Ashleigh was obviously forcing herself to sound cheerful. "As soon as Princess can be moved, she'll be brought here to Whitebrook. She won't be going back to Townsend Acres."

"I hope not, after they practically killed her again," Cindy said fiercely. "Did anyone even suggest it?"

"No. But don't lump all the Townsends with Lavinia, Cindy. Mr. Townsend stayed with me through all of Princess's surgery, for eight hours. He says he feels as bad about what happened to her as I do," Ashleigh said with a sigh. "I don't think that's possible, but I appreciate what he's doing."

"Yeah, Mr. Townsend is okay," Cindy said grudgingly. "But I hate Lavinia."

"Everything's not over for Princess. I mean, maybe it's not. She'll make a wonderful broodmare—if . . . if she tolerates her injury. Of course, that's a big if." Ashleigh buried her face in her hands. "I'm sorry," she said, turning to go. "I'll be glad when Princess is back. I'm sure she'll get better fast with all our love."

"Of course she will," Cindy said quickly. At least she could try to reassure Ashleigh. She looked back at Glory. The big gray was still watching her over the stall door.

After Ashleigh had left, Cindy walked over to Glory's stall and rubbed his forehead. The horse leaned blissfully into her caresses.

"At least you're here and in one piece," Cindy said to him grimly. "Ashleigh always wanted to get Princess away from Townsend Acres and bring her to Whitebrook. But she didn't want her to come this way—Princess may not even be alive."

In her dream that night Cindy was back at the Keeneland racetrack. *"And it's Townsend Princess who blazes the way around the far turn!" the announcer cried. . . .*

Princess was leading, just the way she had been in her last race. This time, though, Cindy wasn't afraid for her. Princess would be fine. "And Townsend Princess comes flying!" the announcer called.

Princess was flying, all right. But to her horror, Cindy saw that Princess was careening on three legs while her fourth leg hung by a thread. And it wasn't Princess's leg anymore—it was Glory's! Cindy began to scream. . . .

She sat bolt upright in bed, clutching the sheet. Cold sweat had broken out on her forehead. "What a terrible nightmare," she gasped.

A waning moon gleamed through her window, turning the furniture and walls ghostly blue-white. Cindy shook her head, trying to drive away the dream. "That really was just a nightmare," she told herself. "Now I'm awake. Nothing has happened to Glory."

Suddenly Cindy knew she had to see him just to make sure. She untangled her legs from the covers and quickly dressed.

The moon faintly illuminated the path as she ran to the training barn. The farm was completely silent, sunk in the night.

Cindy walked down the dark aisle of the barn. She didn't want to turn on the lights and wake up the horses. She would just look in on Glory and make sure he was sleeping peacefully, then go back to bed.

But as she approached Glory's stall, she saw that the big horse was awake too and looking out over the stall door. "Glory?" Cindy whispered. "What is it?"

Glory tossed his elegant head and nickered. In the faint light his dappled coat was almost black.

Why was Glory awake at this hour? Horses didn't sleep as much as people, but all the other horses were asleep. Maybe Glory was just restless.

"What are you trying to tell me? Are you scared of something too?" Cindy asked softly, taking the gray colt's muzzle in her hands.

Glory rubbed his head against her shirt. Well, if neither of them could sleep, she might as well stay awhile. Cindy let herself into the stall and settled on the straw, with her back against the wall. She was definitely tired, even if she wasn't sleepy.

Glory seemed wide awake. He turned quickly around in the stall to face her.

Cindy looked up at him. Glory was so beautiful, he made her heart ache. "We've been through so much together, boy," she said. "I can't let anything happen to you."

Glory stepped over to her and gently blew in her hair. Cindy felt a little calmer. She reached up to touch his velvet nose, then rested her head against the back of the stall. As long as she and Glory were together, they'd be fine.

Hours later Cindy awoke with a jerk. It was still night. For a second the straw under her hands felt strange; then she remembered where she was.

Glory was dipping his muzzle into his feed box, looking for any last bits of grain from his dinner. That was a good sign. Nervous or sick horses didn't usually eat.

Cindy got up, shaking a foot that had fallen asleep. She would like to spend the whole night in the barn, but her parents might notice she wasn't in her bed and they might worry. "Let's both try to sleep, Glory," she said. "Maybe I can ride and you can run when we're exhausted, but I don't want to try it. Okay? Your first race is in less than a week."

The big horse looked at her. Cindy wasn't sure if he'd gotten the message, but maybe Glory had gotten enough sleep already, in the first part of the night.

I know I haven't, Cindy said to herself as she walked back up to the house.

She flopped down on her bed, not bothering to change into her pajamas again. The alarm clock said three-thirty A.M. That gave her just an hour and a half to sleep before she had to get up for chores and to work Glory. Then she had to face Monday morning at school. Cindy turned over on her stomach resolutely.

She tried to think of pleasant things that would help her sleep: mares grazing peacefully in the paddock, the bright-eyed, trustful gaze of foals, the swirl of colors as jockeys rode by in their silks at the track.

One of the jockeys turned into McCauley, and he was riding Princess toward the gate. Cindy's eyes flew open.

Cindy punched the pillow and shut her eyes tight.

Any sleep was better than none, even if she had the nightmare again. Besides, it was only a dream.

But what if it comes true? she thought.

When Cindy awoke, she felt tired and draggy. Her muscles were stiff, as if she'd tensed them all night. *Or maybe I just slept in a stall,* she thought as she clumped down the stairs to the breakfast table.

"Hey, sweetie," Ian greeted her. He was reading the *Daily Racing Form* and sipping coffee. Beth sat at the table too, poring over the newspaper.

"There's your juice on the counter," Beth said. "Blueberry pancakes are coming up."

"I think I'll just skip breakfast and go on down to the barn." Cindy already had her hand on the doorknob.

"Why?" Beth asked. Both her parents looked up in surprise.

"I need to see Glory. I want to make sure he's okay," Cindy blurted.

"Honey, of course he's okay. Don't let what happened to Princess rattle you," Ian said, sounding concerned.

"I won't. I just want to feed Glory right away so that we can get out for his work. I'll eat later," Cindy told Beth, quickly letting herself out before they could quiz her further.

In the barn the horses were all eagerly leaning over their doors, whickering and stamping—except for Glory. The big gray colt wasn't looking out of his stall, anticipating breakfast, the way he always was.

Cindy's steps slowed. "Glory?" she whispered. Had something happened to him after she'd left last night? What if he'd colicked and gone down? Cindy rushed to Glory's stall and flung open the door.

Glory was standing in the back, with his tail to her. He swung around with an alarmed snort.

"Oh, boy, you were still asleep!" Cindy said. She slumped against the side of the stall. "I'm sorry I scared you. But you scared *me.*"

Glory stayed where he was, watching her. "I'm being dumb," Cindy said, stretching out her hand to him. "This is another morning, just like every other one. I'm turning it into a nightmare."

Glory finally wandered over for his morning petting. Cindy gave it to him, then went to the feed room to measure out Glory's grain. When she poured the oats and sweet feed into his box, the big colt pushed his muzzle deep into the food with a huff of pleasure.

"You like that, don't you?" she asked. "And when I brush you, you'll be even happier."

Mike and Gene Reese emerged from the office, talking about Mr. Wonderful's upcoming maiden race at Keeneland, on the same day as Glory's. "It's always hard to tell what will happen in a maiden race," Mr. Reese said. "But I think Mr. Wonderful will outclass the rest of the field."

"I'm looking forward to it," Mike answered. "We've waited a long time for this moment. And after him, we won't have another of Wonder's offspring coming along for two years, assuming everything goes well with her new foal when it's born."

"What's the news on Princess?" Mr. Reese asked.

"Ashleigh spoke to the vet about an hour ago." Mike's voice was grim. "He's very concerned about Princess. She's come out of the sedatives, and she's fighting her confinement. She may not tolerate it much longer."

Cindy stopped brushing Glory. She felt sick. Nobody had to tell her what that meant—Princess would probably have to be put down. Cindy took a deep breath. "I've got a horse to work," she said aloud. "No one else is sitting down and crying because Princess may die."

Ashleigh and Samantha were waiting by the training oval as Cindy led Glory to the gap. "Ready to go with this guy?" Ashleigh asked. Her voice was chipper, but her face looked drawn and sad.

Cindy nodded, and Ashleigh gave her a leg into the saddle. Glory danced sideways, tossing his head and yanking on the bit. Cindy fought down panic. "Stop it," she muttered to herself. Glory would instantly pick up on her tension. If she was afraid of him, he would know it.

"I'm going to take Shining and Mr. Wonderful around," Ashleigh said. "Samantha will coach you, Cindy."

"Great," Cindy said. She knew her voice sounded funny.

Ashleigh walked off to get Shining from Vic.

Samantha looked at Cindy strangely. "Are you all right? I know you're used to working with Ashleigh."

"I'm fine." Cindy didn't know what she could say about her fears for Glory. Samantha would just remind her that getting hurt was a risk both horse and rider took in racing, and not to dwell on it.

"I'd like to shoot for breezing him a half mile today," Samantha said. "But first let's see how his warmup goes."

Cindy clucked to Glory, and the big colt moved out smoothly at a trot. So far, so good. Across the track Cindy saw Ashleigh gallop Shining to the three-eighths pole, then crouch over her neck, letting her out. Shining thundered around the far turn, a gleaming red-and-white streak in the sun, her hooves pounding the loose dirt of the track as she hurtled into the stretch.

"That'll be us breezing in a minute," Cindy told Glory. For the first time, though, she wasn't looking forward to it.

The big colt flicked back an ear, listening, but he still wouldn't settle down. When Cindy asked him for a gallop, he hesitated, then put his head down and launched into an awkward, stiff pace.

I wonder if something's wrong with his legs. Cindy pulled Glory up on the backstretch. The colt angrily shook his head, as if he was trying to tell her that they didn't stop on the track at this part of the work.

"I know," Cindy said. "I'm a chicken today." She ran her hand along Glory's glossy neck and tried to think about the work instead of her fears. Samantha must be wondering what they were doing. "I don't really know what we're doing either," Cindy admitted aloud.

She asked Glory for a gallop again, and this time he responded with an almost smooth gait. They circled the oval, passing Samantha.

"Gallop him around again and breeze him out a quarter," Samantha called.

They swept out of the backstretch. Glory began to extend his gallop, anticipating the breeze starting at the quarter pole. Cindy felt her nervousness return. What if Glory fell apart like Princess? "You're so special, Glory," she whispered. "I'd die if anything happened to you."

Suddenly Glory lurched toward the inside rail. Cindy almost screamed as she slid sideways, nearly losing her seat. The next instant Glory grabbed the bit in his teeth and bolted, running out on the track. A tractor rumbling across the back paddock spooked the colt even more, and he angled back in along the rail. Cindy threw both arms around Glory's neck and barely managed to stay in the saddle.

"Glory, stop!" she cried, desperately trying to think what to do. Where would this crazy ride end? No one could help her—if anyone rode in pursuit, Glory would just go faster. She saw in a blur that the other riders on the track had hastily pulled their horses to the outside rail, trying to stay out of their way.

Cindy worked her way back to a sitting position and clung to Glory's thick mane. The effort of hanging on made her legs ache, but she couldn't fall—Glory might injure himself running loose.

The gray colt roared past the mile marker, then slowed, as he usually did after they passed the gap. "Oh, thank God," Cindy gasped. Apparently Glory felt he had to show her how to do a work this morning.

"What was going on out there?" Samantha called as Cindy trotted Glory toward the gap.

"He spooked." Cindy tried to control the trembling in her legs, but she couldn't. This was terrible—Glory had never acted like that for her. And he was still upset. His neck was lathered and he was tossing his head, jerking the reins through her hands.

Samantha held up the stopwatch. "He did the quarter in twenty-six—not bad for a horse that was zigging and zagging all over the track. Jeez, Cindy, you scared me to death! You both could have gotten hurt."

"I know." Cindy gulped.

Ashleigh rode over on Shining, shaking her head. "Too bad," she said. "Glory really is acting almost schizophrenic. He must be remembering the bad part of his training today—he seemed terrified."

Cindy couldn't stand to hear her beloved colt blamed. "It was my fault," she choked out.

"Don't be so upset, Cindy," Ashleigh said. "We'll lick this. One of Glory's problems is focus. If we could just figure out how to stop him from losing his focus and spooking, we'd have a racehorse. A lot of it seems to have to do with confidence, which he usually has when you ride him."

Cindy blinked back tears. She certainly didn't have much confidence today. Glory might be the next Just Victory, and she was spoiling his chances.

"We need to have a lot of patience with him." Ashleigh looked closely at Glory. "Take him around again—just an easy gallop. We can't end the training session like this."

"Maybe you or Samantha should ride him." The words hurt, but Cindy knew she had to do what was best for Glory.

Ashleigh was silent for a few seconds. "No, he goes best for you. Just don't go to sleep out there."

I certainly wasn't sleeping! Cindy thought. But she nodded. She couldn't give up now.

The roar of a powerful car motor spooked Glory. He skittered sideways, rolling his eyes and yanking on the bit. When Cindy finally got him under control again, she saw Brad and Lavinia getting out of their Ferrari.

"Just what we need," Samantha said grimly.

Cindy felt her cheeks flame. How dare Brad and Lavinia even show up here, after what had happened to Princess?

The Townsends walked over to the training oval. Lavinia was wearing a stylish drop-waist maternity dress and a broad-brimmed sun hat.

"Where's Mr. Wonderful? We want to watch his work," Brad said arrogantly.

At that moment Vic appeared in the doorway of the training barn, leading the chestnut colt.

"Here he comes," Lavinia said. "He's such a nice-looking animal. You can really see his sire in him. Baldasar is one of the most incredible horses Townsend Acres ever bred."

Ashleigh just nodded. "Okay, Cindy, back to work," she said. "Start over—walk, trot, slow gallop once around. I'm afraid Glory's had his breeze for today."

"What was his time?" Lavinia asked.

"Twenty-six." Samantha didn't elaborate.

"Second rate," Lavinia commented. "He isn't nearly as showy looking as Mr. Wonderful, either."

Cindy took Glory back out to the track before she blew a fuse. How could Ashleigh be so calm when the person who had almost killed Princess just strolled onto the farm and started sounding off?

Cindy looked between the gray tips of Glory's ears and tried to concentrate. But either because she was upset, or Glory was still upset, the work went from bad to terrible. Cindy could hardly control the colt. Glory shied at real but ordinary things, imaginary things, and Lavinia's hat, which she took off to fan her face every time they went around in front of her.

"Glory, please don't do this," Cindy whispered. Her arms felt like rubber from hauling on the reins, and her legs were shaking so much she could barely keep her seat. But she knew that horses had to be made to mind, not bargained with. If she didn't show Glory who was boss, he was going to act up. The trouble was, she just couldn't do it today. Cindy rode back to the gap, shaking her head.

"That horse needs to be ridden with a whip to get his mind on business," Brad commented.

Cindy's mouth dropped open in shock. If Glory hadn't been whipped so much in his life, they wouldn't have a problem with him in the first place.

"You're amazing, Brad," Ashleigh said coldly. "You want me to whip a horse the minute he doesn't perform adequately. I guess you've forgotten what happened when you tried that with Wonder. She was so frightened by the whip that we almost didn't have a racehorse at all, never mind a Derby winner."

Brad shrugged. "This horse isn't Wonder. I'll be surprised if he lifts a hoof at the track."

"Brad, if you don't mind, I've got horses to ride and train," Ashleigh said impatiently. "I can't stand here and speculate on every last racehorse's resemblance to Wonder."

"Of course I don't mind." Brad smiled his superior smile. "I just think you could use a couple of pointers. Are you going to take Mr. Wonderful around or not? I've got an appointment at eight."

They act like they own Mr. Wonderful and everything on the place. Cindy couldn't believe it.

Without a word, Ashleigh mounted the chestnut colt. "Just trot Glory while I work this guy," she said to Cindy. "Then I'll take Glory around." Ashleigh must have seen the expression on Cindy's face because she added, "I'd meant to anyway, this close to race day."

"All right," Cindy said unhappily. She still felt in disgrace. At least Ashleigh was still talking about Glory's race day as if there was going to be one.

Ashleigh took Mr. Wonderful around. The colt performed perfectly, doing exactly as Ashleigh asked in his warmups, then breezing out a fast, graceful quarter. Ashleigh was the picture of easy competence. Cindy felt even worse.

Ashleigh was smiling as she rode over to them.

"You should breeze him three eighths, not a quarter," Brad called. "He needs to be sharp."

"Day after tomorrow," Ashleigh said curtly. "I don't want to make him run a blowout now." Cindy knew that a blowout was a fast work close to the time of a race, intended to bring a horse up to peak.

Well, at this rate no one would be worrying about when Glory should do a blowout. The gray colt was standing quietly under Cindy now, lightly tugging at the reins. Probably he was wondering if they were going back to the barn soon.

Brad stepped away from the rail. "We'll be here tomorrow to watch Mr. Wonderful work," he said. "I want to stay on top of his game."

"It's your option." Ashleigh shrugged.

Speechless, Cindy watched as Brad and Lavinia swaggered to their Ferrari and drove off.

"Okay, I'll take Glory around now," Ashleigh said, handing off Mr. Wonderful to Vic. "Sammy, why don't you ride Matchless with us? Maybe Glory will settle down if he has company."

Cindy dismounted from Glory, feeling utterly defeated. She slowly patted the big colt's shoulder. Glory leaned around and nudged her, as if he shared her distress.

"What's the matter, Cindy?" Samantha asked gently. "Glory was doing great for you until today."

"It's my riding, I guess," Cindy said, almost in tears from the disappointment of the bad work and the stress of seeing the Townsends. "I just don't have the experience to make Glory do what I want."

"I might have given you the wrong instructions at the beginning of the work," Samantha said. "I'm not that experienced a trainer. I trained Shining, but she's Wonder's half sister—maybe I just couldn't go wrong with her."

"It's not an accident that Shining is a great racehorse," Cindy protested.

"Stop all this self-doubting, you two," Ashleigh said. "Don't you remember, Sammy, how I felt when Charlie died and I had to train Pride for the biggest races of his life all by myself? But I did know what to do. The hardest part was to make myself believe that."

"Okay," Samantha said with a wry smile. "At least the Townsends have taken off. That should help."

Cindy watched enviously as the two young women headed Glory and Matchless down the middle of the track. She wanted so much to be on Glory—she *belonged* on Glory. But he seemed to be minding Ashleigh better.

"Now he's going pretty well," Ashleigh said when they passed Cindy for the first time. "Let's try a quarter-mile breeze with them, Sammy. I hope it doesn't take too much out of Glory, but I don't want the memory of that first, bad breeze to stick in his mind."

Ashleigh and Samantha galloped to the quarter pole. At the same instant the two riders rose over the horses' necks, urging them forward.

Matchless surged ahead but Glory hung back, dropping to a length behind, then several lengths. "Glory, what's *wrong*?" Cindy muttered through clenched teeth. "You can do better than that!"

The gray colt slowly picked up speed, closing the gap to the other horse, but he still seemed reluctant. Probably Ashleigh was doing some expert riding to get Glory to run at all, Cindy thought. He would never catch the other colt at this rate.

But Glory wasn't out of it yet. Suddenly he seemed to find his stride, and Cindy's heart leapt as the big gray rolled on faster and faster, eating into the other horse's lead. The colts flashed past the mile marker, with Glory a nose behind but still gaining. Ashleigh rode him back over to Cindy.

"He kicked in, but too late," Ashleigh said, dismounting and handing Glory's reins to Cindy. "He just needs work. I think we've still got time before the race."

Maybe—or maybe Ashleigh's only saying that so I won't feel so bad, Cindy thought. "Thanks, Ashleigh," she said.

Ashleigh nodded, her mind obviously already elsewhere. Cindy led Glory off the oval. Mike and his dad were just coming out of the stallion barn, still talking. Len and Vic's attention was riveted on Seattle Stormcloud, a two-year-old starting her work. No one gave Cindy or Glory a second glance.

Glory stopped and turned to look at the track.

"I know," Cindy said. "If we don't do better than that next time, we won't be going back."

THE SMITHS' TRUCK WAS PARKED IN THE STABLE YARD WHEN Cindy trudged up the drive from the school bus that afternoon. Cindy groaned aloud. "I don't need *them* today," she muttered. Dr. Smith had to come out to look at Blues King, but why did Max keep showing up?

This day had gone so badly, she didn't need the Smiths to ruin the rest of it. After the dismal work that morning with Glory, Cindy had trouble concentrating in school, and Mr. Daniels had spoken sharply to her twice about daydreaming. Cindy had been mortified—usually she was Mr. Daniels's pet. Of course Max had made fun of her about it.

"I can really depend on Max to come through," Cindy said to herself as she stomped into the house.

Beth was in the kitchen, cutting up vegetables, cheese, and chicken for a large chef's salad. "Hi," she said. "How was school?"

"Fine." Cindy shrugged and headed for the stairs. It would take an hour to explain everything that had gone wrong at school today, and she wanted to get out to the barn as soon as possible. But how could she avoid Max?

Cindy grabbed jeans and a T-shirt out of a drawer. After this morning's disaster on the track, she needed to see Glory—to run her hands through his thick, soft mane and along his silky coat and talk to him until she felt like they were themselves again.

Cindy pounded down the stairs and out the door. "Glory has to be exercised if there's any hope of him racing Saturday," she said to herself as she walked to the barn. "So I'll take him out, the way I meant to before I saw that the Smiths were here. If Max tries to tag along, I'll just have to be rude and tell him he can't come."

Besides, Max didn't want to ride with her. It was just her dad and his mom who kept trying to force them to be together.

Glory whinnied shrilly when he saw her. The Smiths were nowhere in sight.

"Hush, boy." Cindy quickly brought the gray out to the crossties and began to brush him down. "Max and his mom must be in one of the other barns. Maybe if we hurry, we can sneak out before they see us."

Glory gave a low, throaty whinny, as if he understood. Cindy ran to the tack room to get Glory's saddle and bridle. She tacked him up so fast, if it had been a timed event she would have won it. She mounted up and trotted by the barns.

Cindy relaxed. *Made it.*

The next second Max Smith rode around the corner of the stallion barn on Ruling Spirit, one of the older Thoroughbred exercise horses.

Cindy's mouth dropped open. Before she could gallop Glory off, her dad and Dr. Smith walked out of the barn.

"Oh, Cindy," Ian hailed her. "I knew you'd be out to ride Glory, so we tacked up Spirit for Max. Dr. Smith says Max is really anxious to ride since his horse has been out of commission for so long."

"No, he isn't," Cindy said bluntly. She had never been so rude in her life, and she was sorry to embarrass her dad, but even looking at Max reminded Cindy of his barbs today in school. Besides, her dad wasn't doing Max a favor, although he thought he was—Dr. Smith had probably made Max get on that horse.

"I'd like to go for a ride," Max said suddenly.

Cindy looked at him in surprise. He seemed to mean it. She thought fast. She couldn't sit here all afternoon, trying to keep Max from coming with her, when Glory needed exercise so much. "Okay," she said, not very graciously. "But I'm working this horse, not just walking around the woods."

"Fine." Max shrugged. "I'm up for a hard ride."

"Don't hurry," Dr. Smith called. "I'm going on a call at a farm nearby. I won't be back for an hour or two."

Great. Cindy silently led the way to the lane behind the front paddocks. Maybe if she and Max just rode and didn't talk, they'd get along fine.

In one of the paddocks the mares were out with their young foals. Four had been born at Whitebrook so far this year. Cindy smiled as two of the youngsters frolicked around the paddock, awkwardly kicking up their long, slender legs. The other two foals were very seriously nursing and energetically flicking their brush tails.

Max caught up to Cindy. "What horses are those?"

Cindy named them, effortlessly reciting pedigrees. Max appeared impressed. "Whitebrook's a famous breeding farm," he commented.

"Yeah, it is," Cindy agreed. "There's Ashleigh's Wonder, our most famous mare," she said, pointing. Wonder was watching them from the middle of a field. She hadn't had her foal yet, although it was due any day now. Wonder didn't move. She was so big, she was probably barely capable of it.

Max studied Wonder. "Wow," he said. "So that's your Derby winner, huh?"

"Her foals are winners too. I bet her daughter, Townsend Princess, would have won the Derby this year if she hadn't gotten hurt." Cindy abruptly turned Glory and headed up the lane. She didn't want to think about Princess.

The sun poked out from behind a giant swirl of cloud, lighting Max's dark hair and turning the grassy fields emerald as they rode along. Cindy felt strange being out on the familiar trails with Max instead of Samantha or Heather.

"When does Glory race?" Max asked.

"This weekend." Cindy decided not to say anything about her fears that Glory wouldn't be racing at all. "Let's trot," she added.

"Okay." Max put Ruling Spirit into the faster gait with an almost imperceptible motion of his legs. Cindy followed on Glory. She noticed that Max was sitting to the trot, not posting, and moved easily with the horse, showing the skill of the experienced rider. He looked good, Cindy had to admit.

They stopped Glory and Spirit behind the back paddock. The horses had been rotated out of the paddock to rest it, and daisies dotted the soft new bluegrass. "What kind of horse do you have?" Cindy asked.

"A Thoroughbred."

Cindy was startled. Not that it was so unusual for someone to have a Thoroughbred in Kentucky horse country—probably half the kids at school did—but Cindy had never thought she and Max had anything in common, much less a love of horses.

Glory snatched a mouthful of leaves from a nearby bush. Cindy sat back in the saddle, enjoying for a moment the sunlight sparkling off a spiderweb and the chattering of a gray squirrel in a tree above them. Then she reminded herself that she and Glory had work to do.

"I need to gallop him," she said. "He's got to stay in shape for his first race this Saturday—if he races. His works haven't been all that good lately."

Why did I tell Max that? she thought with horror. "If

you laugh, I'm taking off right across the meadow," she said fiercely. "You can find your own way home. Spirit can't keep up with Glory."

"I'll bet not too many horses can," Max said. He actually wasn't jeering.

"Sometimes I wonder if *any* horse can." Cindy blew out a breath. "When Glory runs his best, he's awesome. And that's usually for me, until . . . well, until Princess broke her leg again. That could so easily happen to Glory. Now I almost don't want him to run."

"I sometimes get pretty attached to the horses my mom treats," Max said. "For months we worked on Attaché, a stallion over at Stanton Farm who had navicular. My mom managed to keep him going for one more breeding season, but his feet finally disintegrated, and she had to put him down. So I guess I know how you feel about Princess."

"How long have you been riding?" Cindy asked to change the subject.

"Oh—almost since I was born." Max shrugged. "We've always had a couple of horses. Most of them are retired Thoroughbreds that my mom reconditioned. My dad used to help her and sell some of them, but my parents got divorced about five years ago, and he lives in Seattle now."

Max suddenly looked as though he wished he hadn't told her that. Maybe he was afraid she would laugh, like she'd been when she told him about Glory.

"Let's canter," she said, not waiting for Max's reply. Glory sprang forward at her signal.

Max charged after her on Ruling Spirit. "Hey, you're not a bad rider—at this slow pace!" he called.

That sounded more like the Max she knew. "So we'll turn at the next lane and gallop out a mile!" she yelled back. "*If* you can keep up!"

"Don't worry about me!"

Cindy slowed Glory to make the right-angle turn into the galloping lane. Glory snorted and tugged at the reins. He knew what was coming.

The mile-long lane was covered with thick grass, blowing gently in the light breeze. Max guided Ruling Spirit beside her.

"Ready, set, go!" he said, and at the same instant they heeled their horses into a gallop.

Max was asking Spirit to give his all, Cindy saw, but the retired Thoroughbred didn't stand a chance against Glory. Glory was flying. Cindy bent low over the colt's neck, half closing her eyes against the blaze of the sinking sun as the gray colt effortlessly bounded along the lane. She felt as if they could take off on the red-ribbon highways of the clouds.

At the end of the lane Cindy pulled Glory up and tried to catch her breath. Max galloped up a few seconds later, his eyes shining. "Wow—Glory's really fast! That was great!"

Cindy glanced over at him. That *had* been fun. Max was a much bolder rider than Heather. He rode the way Cindy did herself.

"But next time you can give me a decent horse and I'll win the race," Max added.

"I doubt it," Cindy said with a smile.

"Maybe if it was a *very* decent horse."

"In a couple of years Wonder's new son or daughter will be ready to ride. That's the only horse I can think of who might be able to catch Glory."

"I'll stay tuned." Max rolled his eyes.

"I guess we'd better take the horses back to feed them," Cindy said. It was getting late. The setting sun outlined the patchy clouds on the horizon in red, as if they were pieces of a puzzle.

Glory turned in the direction of home without being asked, clearly thinking about his dinner too.

"Listen, thanks for letting me ride," Max said as they walked the horses back toward the farm.

"No problem." Cindy felt uncomfortable. She really wouldn't mind if he came again—Max was a dynamite rider. But he hadn't exactly apologized for his behavior toward her in school.

He's not so bad when he's on a horse, though, she thought.

"OKAY, GLORY, WE HAVE TO DO THINGS RIGHT TODAY," Cindy said to the big colt the next morning. That was an understatement. If Glory put in another bad work, Ashleigh would almost certainly scratch him from his first race, in just four days. Today was their last chance.

Glory hung back in his stall, and Cindy's heart sank. He knew they were going out for a work—and he didn't like it. The gray colt looked at her, almost timidly.

"I promise it's okay," Cindy said, clipping on a lead line. "Not all works are bad, remember?" Glory hesitated, then stepped out of the stall after her.

"I have to stop worrying," Cindy murmured. "I'm scaring you too." She put the colt in crossties and quickly tacked him up, trying to push thoughts of broken legs and other track catastrophes from her mind.

"What happened to Princess just won't happen to you," she told Glory. But in her heart she knew it could—or any of a thousand other things. Cindy reached up to unclip Glory, then dropped her hand. She just didn't want him to go out there.

"Oh, Glory," she whispered, putting her arms around the horse's neck. "I want what's best for you. I just don't know what that is."

She heard the sound of boots on the concrete aisle and looked up to see Ashleigh.

Ashleigh nodded a greeting, then leaned against Glory's stall door. Cindy reluctantly joined her. She had a feeling she was going to get yelled at. Cindy knew she should have had Glory out to the oval by now, and Ashleigh had better things to do than chase down exercise riders. Glory craned his neck toward them, as if he intended to participate in the conversation.

"Okay," Ashleigh said. "Out with it—what's wrong?"

"I can't forget the horrible scene at the track with Princess," Cindy blurted. "What if something like that happens to Glory?"

Ashleigh frowned. "I thought Glory's bad work yesterday had something to do with how you were feeling," she said.

Cindy bit a fingernail. "I'm not acting very professional, am I?"

"Don't feel bad about it." Ashleigh shook her head. "So far, Glory has done his best with you riding. He's put his old fears of the track behind him for you. But when you're afraid, he is. You've got to put the past behind you too. You've got to get over what happened to Princess."

"I don't think I ever will." Cindy looked over at Ashleigh. "Can you?" she asked softly.

Ashleigh swallowed. "No one loves Princess more than I do," she said after a moment. "But in her last race, Princess ran her heart out. She ended her career running, doing what she loved to do. No one can have any regrets about it—not really." Ashleigh sighed deeply. "We couldn't have done anything differently. And although we would have had to accept either outcome, I really think Princess is going to make it. We'll be bringing her home soon. So it's time to move on."

Cindy hesitated, thinking of Princess's agony on the track.

"Sometimes with a lot of hard work and good care horses make it through injury, kind of the way your friend Mandy did," Ashleigh said. "Samantha told me about that. Mandy was badly hurt, but she's going to recover. Princess won't, not entirely. So her life will have to take a new direction. Not every story has a completely happy ending, Cindy."

Cindy took a deep breath, then nodded.

"Now get out there and ride that horse the way he's supposed to be ridden." Ashleigh smiled.

"Okay." Cindy pushed herself off the stall door. What Ashleigh had said made sense. Cindy still didn't feel quite right about riding Glory, but she knew she had to try for his sake, and because Ashleigh expected her to.

Glory was still watching her. "All right, big guy," Cindy said. "Today we'll show them."

Last night a light rain had fallen, and the day was overcast. Cindy slogged along the path to the training oval with Glory, trying not to think how muddy the track would be. Glory had never minded running in mud, the way Princess had, but the chance for an accident was greater on a muddy track for any horse. Cindy felt her old fears start up again.

Samantha was cantering Mr. Wonderful on the backstretch, and a couple of other horses were moving around the oval through the fog. Cindy saw her dad standing at the rail in a poncho. She knew he was watching her.

"We've got to move Glory out today," Ashleigh called as Cindy put the colt through his warm-up paces. "Two laps at a gallop, then a quarter-mile breeze."

Glory easily moved into a gallop, his hooves churning the thick mud. "We'll go for a good ride just like with Max and Spirit yesterday," Cindy said reassuringly to herself as much as to Glory. "Nothing to it."

They lapped the track and swung around the first turn. Cindy looked ahead to the quarter pole, on the other side of the track. Fear tightened her throat. *I've got to run him there,* she thought. *But I can't!*

Almost instantly Glory slowed and jumped slightly toward the rail. "Don't be scared!" Cindy said desperately. "You love to run!"

The big colt's ears flicked back. The quarter pole loomed. It was now or never.

"Good," Cindy said quickly. "You're listening to me. You're asking what I really want you to do. Now I know. I want you to run faster than you've ever run before. I want you to run faster than *any* horse has ever run, including your grandsire Just Victory."

The quarter pole flashed by. "Go!" Cindy cried, crouching over Glory's neck and grabbing a handful of his thick mane.

She could feel the big horse hesitating, then he gathered his legs beneath him and surged ahead. Cindy threw back her head, relishing the damp, chilly wind on her face. The mud wasn't slowing Glory at all. He was doing more than running—she knew she'd never be closer to flying than this. Cindy could feel the gray colt's love of speed, the sudden freedom of his movements. Cindy wasn't afraid anymore. She only felt a sense of bliss and awe.

Samantha and Ashleigh were yelling something at her as she and Glory whipped by the gap, but the wind was pounding in her ears and she could barely hear. Cindy circled Glory back to them at a canter, patting the colt's dappled neck. "Fantastic, boy!" she said. "Unbelievable!"

"I wonder if you know how unbelievable!" Ashleigh grinned and held up the stopwatch. "Suddenly I'm confident about race day."

"Twenty-two and change for the quarter is making me comfortable too," Samantha said happily.

"Princess, you're home!" Cindy dropped her pitchfork and rushed to the doorway of the training barn after school that afternoon. Heather dumped a last load of straw in Mr. Wonderful's stall and ran after her.

The beautiful mare limped slowly down the ramp of Whitebrook's two-horse trailer, guided carefully on either side by Ashleigh and Len. Mike jumped out of the truck cab.

"How'd she travel?" Len asked.

"Fine," Mike said. "I took it slow and easy."

Princess threw up her head and whinnied. After a moment an answering call came from the mares' barn. Cindy thought she recognized Wonder's voice.

"Princess is still gorgeous," Heather said softly.

"Yeah, she is." Cindy couldn't stop smiling.

"Come on, girl," Ashleigh said. "Let's get you settled."

Cindy felt a little catch in her throat as Ashleigh led Princess into the mares' barn—not the training barn, where the horses worked on a tight training schedule toward the excitement of race day. All that was over for Princess. The mares' barn was much more quiet and sedate, with the only miracle moment the birth of the foals in the spring.

Cindy and Heather followed Princess into the barn. Len opened a stall door and eased Princess inside. Two stalls down, Wonder stopped eating and looked over her door.

Ashleigh's right. Everything isn't over for Princess, Cindy told herself firmly. *How can being in the same barn with Wonder be anything but good?*

"Finally Wonder, Pride, Mr. Wonderful, and Princess are on our farm," Ashleigh said to Mike. "Isn't that great?" Tears filled her eyes.

Mike squeezed Ashleigh's shoulder. "A new beginning," he said.

"I know." Ashleigh bit her lip.

Cindy went over to Princess's stall. The mare bent her head and blew softly in Cindy's hair. Cindy reached up to rub Princess's white star.

Wonder was still watching them from her stall. Cindy gazed thoughtfully at the two beautiful mares. They looked so much alike. They had run alike, too.

Cindy remembered Princess's last race, and the moments of triumph before the tragedy in the stretch. "I don't think Wonder and Princess both broke bones because their legs are weak," she said. "They really did try harder than the other horses, didn't they?"

"I'm sure of it," Ashleigh answered quietly.

Heather and Cindy left Ashleigh in the barn, still looking at Princess. "So what do you want to do now?" Cindy asked her friend.

"I don't know. Tell me one more time—you went for a trail ride with Max Smith yesterday?" Heather laughed. Cindy had finally told Heather about the ride on the bus home from school, but she had refused to elaborate.

"His mother made him go with me. But it wasn't as terrible as you might think—he can really ride."

Heather batted her eyes. "Didn't I catch you actually being nice to him in science class today?"

"*No*—he just didn't bug me for once."

"Maybe he's getting tired of it."

"I hope so." Cindy felt uncomfortable. "You're not going to believe this, but Samantha thinks he likes me."

"I think Samantha's right." Heather laughed again.

"Way to go, Glory!" Ashleigh shouted, raising a fist in the air. She rode the big gray off the Keeneland track to where Cindy and Samantha waited at the gap. They'd vanned Glory over this morning to work him on the actual race surface. In just three days he'd be running on it.

"That last eighth was good," Ashleigh said, dismounting. "He was a little shaky in the first."

"Atta boy," Cindy said, taking Glory's reins and patting the big colt's neck. He deserved praise for the second eighth of a mile, if not the first. Glory really hadn't kicked in during that first eighth. He'd been up to his old tricks: lagging back, spooking from imaginary things.

"What was his time?" Ashleigh asked.

"Twenty-four for the quarter," Cindy said, looking at the stopwatch.

"That's about what I thought, but I'll get his time from the official clocker too." Cindy knew that Ashleigh had notified the track clocker that she would be breezing Glory, and he would have timed it.

Ashleigh looked down at Cindy. "What was his time for the second eighth?"

"Eleven point five." Cindy held her breath. Was that good enough? Glory rubbed his head urgently against her shoulder, as if he was anxious to know too.

"I'll just have to hope he's more consistent on Saturday." Ashleigh took off her helmet and shook out her hair. "That's going to be what decides the race for this guy. Sammy, I'll tell the clocker I'm going to breeze Mr. Wonderful now."

Vic collected Glory and led him back toward the barn. Cindy stayed to watch Mr. Wonderful. She almost felt like he was Glory's competition, although that was silly. Of course she wanted both horses to win, and they weren't even racing together.

Minutes later Ashleigh and the chestnut colt stepped onto the track. Mr. Wonderful looked alert but gentlemanly, the way he always did.

"Twenty-three seconds and change for the quarter, twelve for the last eighth," Samantha called when Mr. Wonderful roared past the mile marker. "He's material for the classic races," she said to Cindy. "Maybe next year Whitebrook will have an entry in the Derby, Preakness, and Belmont."

"That'd be great," Cindy agreed. She rested her arms on the rail and looked thoughtfully out at the track. Mr. Wonderful had just put in an impressive work. But Glory had done his last eighth of a mile faster—and he'd been gaining speed at the end.

The next day after school Cindy almost ran into Max as she was dashing for the bus home. "Excuse me," she said, trying to sound civil.

"That's okay," Max answered.

Ever since she'd taken him riding, Max had been friendly to her in school. Cindy had thought a couple of times since that if she'd known a ride on a Thoroughbred would turn Max into a nice guy, she could have saved herself a lot of grief by hitting the trails with him sooner.

Cindy flushed. She still didn't really feel comfortable with the new Max. Heather was waving from the bus steps, and Cindy waved back. "Well, I have to catch the bus," she said.

Max raised an eyebrow. "Can I ask you something?"

"Glory's at the track," Cindy said in a rush. "So I guess I won't be going riding for a while."

"I know, I know. Hey, good luck with him Saturday." Max looked serious. "I really think he'll pound the competition."

Cindy stared back at him. "Thanks."

Max shrugged. "Anyway, I just wanted to ask you if you'd like to come with me and my mom on her rounds sometime. She said it's okay."

"I'd love that!" Cindy said excitedly, before she had a chance to realize what she was saying. "Maybe sometime next week?"

Max nodded. "See you," he said, and dived for his own bus.

"I'll bet he lives in a zoo," Heather said when Cindy told her on the bus about Max's invitation.

"Maybe, since his mom's a vet." Cindy laughed. "I'd really like to go with Dr. Smith on her rounds, though, since I might want to be a vet someday. I guess I told Max that."

"I thought you wanted to be a jockey," Heather said.

"Maybe. I'm not very tall now, but it depends on how much I grow. And I haven't worked with very many horses yet, just Glory." Cindy frowned. "I don't know when my dad or Ashleigh will want me to work any of the others—I'm still pretty young even to be an exercise rider. I guess in a way Glory's problems are a good thing. If he went perfectly, Samantha or somebody else would ride him."

"I haven't got the nerve to ride Thoroughbreds," Heather said. "I'll just draw you riding to victory."

"You'll be a famous artist," Cindy assured her.

"I will be after I draw Glory winning at the Breeders' Cup," Heather said firmly.

CINDY SAT AT THE BREAKFAST TABLE ON THE DAY OF GLORY'S first race, crumbling a piece of toast and staring out the kitchen window at the overcast sky. The rain had stopped, but the sky had dumped about an inch on the ground last night. Cindy's parents and Samantha sat across from her, talking about the steeplechase that Sierra had impressively won yesterday. But Cindy could only think about Glory.

Glory would run at three this afternoon, and it was barely four thirty in the morning now. Cindy wondered what she would be thinking in twelve hours, after the race. When she was sitting here tonight, would she be celebrating Glory's victory or utterly miserable because he lost?

"The excitement is killing me," Beth said, smiling at Cindy. "Mr. Wonderful *and* Glory are running in their maidens."

Cindy smiled back, but her thoughts were already at Keeneland. She hoped Glory was still doing all right, after two nights away from home at the track. She'd loaded up Imp in the van with him, so the big colt would have his cat friend for company.

"Ready to go?" Mr. McLean asked, setting his breakfast dishes in the sink. "Ashleigh and Mike will drive over in their car and meet us at the track."

Cindy nodded and ran upstairs to get a jacket. "Please let the weather clear up so the track isn't a mud mess," she muttered. "Glory and Mr. Wonderful will have enough to deal with in their first race without that."

But as they drove the short distance to Keeneland, Cindy could see that she wouldn't get her wish. The sky lightened to a lustrous pearl gray, but the sun wasn't sizzling—the way it would have to be to dry the ground much by afternoon. Cindy bit a fingernail. She was trying not to think it, but the track had been muddy for Princess's last race. That could be a very bad sign.

At the Whitebrook stabling, Cindy looked into Glory's stall. The gray colt was poking at his straw bedding with a hoof. When he saw Cindy, he whinnied happily.

"I haven't abandoned you," Cindy reassured him, slipping inside the stall. The colt immediately checked her back pocket for treats and was rewarded with a carrot.

Cindy stayed with Glory most of the morning, leaving the barn only to buy a plate of nachos for brunch at the track kitchen. Ashleigh, Mike, Mr. Reese, and Ian roamed the shed rows and talked to other owners and trainers. As Cindy walked back down the barn aisle, carrying her food, she overheard her dad talking to a couple of other trainers she recognized from Oakridge Meadows, a farm near Whitebrook.

"We've got big hopes for the colt," Ian said. "Today may not be a true test of his speed, with the track condition, but I think he'll show us what he's got."

"My money's on him," said one of the other trainers, a small, compact man. Cindy knew he was a former jockey.

"If Mr. Wonderful has got a tenth of Ashleigh's Wonder or Wonder's Pride's ability, this is going to be a race to remember," said the other trainer, a pudgy man chewing on an unlit cigar.

The trainers weren't talking about Glory. Mr. Wonderful was definitely the star Whitebrook attraction. *But only until Glory races,* Cindy told herself firmly, letting herself back into Glory's stall.

"I'm going to brush you until you're so shiny, Lavinia Townsend and everyone else watching will fall out of their chairs when they see how beautiful you are," Cindy told him, moving a dandy brush over Glory's dappled coat.

Glory reached around and grabbed the brush with his teeth. "Thanks, but I don't need help," Cindy said, laughing as she pulled the brush away from him. She managed to get the big colt groomed, despite Glory's repeated efforts to yank the brush away again.

"Let's head up to our seats," Ian said as Cindy was putting away her grooming tools in Glory's tack trunk. "It's almost post time."

Mr. Wonderful was running in the first race on the card, a six-furlong sprint for maiden two-year-olds. Cindy joined Beth, Samantha, and Mike in the grandstand and watched with growing excitement as Ashleigh jogged the honey-colored colt out to the track for the post parade.

He really looked like Wonder—all of Wonder's foals looked like her. But this race would show if he had her speed and heart.

A pale sun shone through scattered high clouds, but the track was still listed as muddy. "How do you think Mr. Wonderful will do in the mud?" Samantha asked Ian.

"He didn't seem to like it much in his workouts. But I'm not sure if he was just startled by it or if he was having trouble running," Ian answered. "Today we'll find out."

Samantha nodded, narrowing her eyes thoughtfully as she gazed at the track.

Mr. Wonderful loaded quietly into the number-five position in the gate. One of the seven other young horses in the race reared up in the gate, almost going over backward. A track attendant climbed up on the gate partition to hold the horse's bridle.

There was a moment of silence, as if the crowd were holding its breath. The next second eight powerful horses roared out of the gate. Mr. Wonderful was running last.

"He bumped the gate," Samantha said tersely. "Now he can't find his stride in the mud."

"He's not giving up!" Cindy had to shout over the noise of the cheering spectators.

"No, he's got too much heart for that!"

Cindy watched with a lump in her throat as Mr. Wonderful battled back, passing the last two horses in the field. She didn't think he could catch the others. The frontrunners had opened up a five-length lead on him, and the short race was already half over.

Mr. Wonderful passed two more horses easily. But a wall of three horses churned the muddy track in front of him.

"He doesn't have anywhere to go," Ian yelled.

"Ashleigh's taking him around three wide on the turn," Samantha yelled back. Showing amazing speed, Mr. Wonderful put away the three horses and moved up fast on the leader, a big bay called Dancer's Perfection.

The horses thundered into the stretch. Dancer's jockey glanced over his shoulder, saw Mr. Wonderful, and went for his whip. Mr. Wonderful fought through the mud, slowly gaining, but he was out of ground. Dancer shot under the wire to win by a nose.

"Darn!" Samantha cried. "Mr. Wonderful just about caught him."

Now it's up to Glory to win for Whitebrook, Cindy thought.

"Mr. Wonderful ran a good race," Mike said. "We can't fault his performance, given the way the race played out."

Still, everyone from Whitebrook looked disappointed as they walked to the track. The chestnut colt had come so close to his first victory.

A few minutes later Ashleigh led a still blowing, mud-spattered Mr. Wonderful through the gap.

"That is one muddy horse," Beth said, smiling.

"I took some myself." Ashleigh looked for a second at her mud-caked silks.

"What did you think of his performance?" Mike asked as Vic took Mr. Wonderful to sponge him off and cool him out.

"We can't tell from this first race if he'll go the distance, but it's a great start," Ashleigh said. "I don't think he really minded the mud, either. If he hadn't bumped the gate, he would have run decently in it."

"That was my impression too." Mike nodded.

Glory likes mud and puddles, Cindy thought. At least he did at home, on the trail. Nobody had ever worked Glory on a surface as sloppy as this one, though. He would be slipping, and mud from the hooves of the other horses would fly in his face unless Ashleigh took him straight to the front. That wasn't always possible in a race.

"Time to get Glory ready," Ashleigh said. "I'm going to get cleaned up, even if I only stay that way for an hour before I ride again."

"We'll come with you partway," Mike said. "I'd like to finish talking to that breeder from Versailles I met earlier. He's got a filly I wouldn't mind adding to our stock."

"I'll stay with Glory," Cindy said.

"We'll join you in a few minutes," Samantha said. "Okay?"

"Sure." Cindy nodded. She wanted to be alone with Glory for a little while anyway, to give him a pep talk.

When she looked in on him, the gray horse was rolling in his stall, luxuriously scratching his back. At least he wasn't nervous, Cindy thought. But then, he didn't know what was coming.

The big colt jumped up, shaking himself. "Okay, now you've spoiled all my brushing work," Cindy scolded. "I'll have to start over."

She brushed Glory's coat again, rubbing it to a shine with a soft rag. Then she combed Glory's long, silky tail, freeing it of the last bits of straw. He was set.

Cindy stepped outside the barn to look at the weather. Dark clouds were blowing in from the west, obscuring the tepid sun. Cindy rubbed her aching arm, the one she'd broken last summer. Pain in her arm was a pretty good indicator of increasing dampness in the air.

Rain would make the track even more dangerous. Cindy took a deep breath, pushing away the memories of Princess. Glory wasn't going to break anything today—he was going to run the race of his life.

Glory looked out of his stall, probably wondering where she was.

"Just a minute, boy." Suddenly Cindy was incredibly nervous. So much depended on this race. She had to calm down before she went in Glory's stall—she'd make him nervous too.

"Get it together," Cindy ordered herself. Glory needed her. The most critical part of Glory's race might be just calming him enough to run his best.

"That horse hasn't got what it takes to race," Brad Townsend said, walking up from behind Cindy to Glory's stall.

Glory backed away from the door with a loud snort.

"Don't scare him," Cindy said. Her mind was racing. Nobody else from Whitebrook was around, and she'd never had to deal with Brad alone. What was he doing here? Mr. Wonderful wasn't even back in the barn—Vic was still cooling him out.

"Scare him even more than he already is—make him psychotic." Brad laughed.

Cindy didn't know what to do. Brad was a grown-up, and she couldn't just order him away from Glory's stall, the way Ashleigh would. Cindy looked around for help, but the barn was still deserted.

"I know that horse has decent breeding," Brad said, backing away a pace from Glory's stall. He scrutinized the colt intently.

Cindy gave a sigh of relief. Maybe Glory would settle down now if Brad didn't come too close.

"He's a mess, though," Brad continued. "Ashleigh should scratch him from this race and turn him into a pleasure horse. He's so unpredictable, he's a danger to the other jockeys and horses."

"I disagree," said a deep voice behind them.

Cindy turned quickly. She could hardly believe her

eyes, but Ben Cavell stood there. "Ben, I'm so glad you're here!" she said.

Brad nodded. "Ben," he said casually. "Nice to see you." Cindy noticed how much more civil Brad's tone was to the famous trainer than to her.

"This horse has far more talent than any horse in his race today. As I think you know," Ben added.

Brad shrugged. "Time will tell," he said. "Anyway, I have things to do. See you around, Ben." Cindy didn't care that Brad pointedly ignored her, as long as he left.

"Are you going to watch Glory's race?" Cindy asked Ben.

"Wouldn't miss it." Ben leaned against Glory's stall door. The big gray happily nudged him. He obviously remembered his old friend.

"I'm getting awfully nervous," Cindy confessed. "Brad was making it worse for Glory and me. I don't know why he was here."

"Young Townsend is interested in Glory. He's fairly knowledgeable about horses, and he wanted to check him out."

"Why would he care about Glory?" Cindy asked.

"Because he thinks the colt will win his race—and not just this one."

"I hope so." Cindy swallowed nervously.

"A lot's riding on this race for the colt," Ben acknowledged. "But he's ready."

"How do you know?" Cindy wondered for a second if Ben could communicate with Glory by telepathy.

"Word travels fast. I saw his clockings here."

"No one else thought they were that great."

"I'll bet Glory's trainer was impressed, although she may still be cautious about him," Ben said. "The second eighth was remarkable. And the track was playing slow."

"Glory runs incredibly fast, but we still haven't gotten him over spooking at things," Cindy said in a rush. "I wanted to ask you—"

"A word to the wise," Ben said.

"What?" Cindy looked at him in surprise.

"If Glory starts that spooking business, tell the jockey to talk to him," Ben said. "Sometimes a kind word snaps him out of it. The worst thing to do would be whip him. It's a mental thing with him."

"Thanks," Cindy said gratefully. "I'll tell Ashleigh."

Ben rose. "I'm going to talk to the jockey about a colt I'm running in the fifth race. I've got a little something for you," he said gruffly, handing her a small package wrapped in tissue paper. "A good-luck charm, you might say. Open it before Glory's race. There's some history to it—I'll explain someday."

"Bye—and thanks a lot, Ben!" Cindy looked back at Glory. The gray colt was watching the door Ben had disappeared through. "You heard him," she said. "Now we'd both better do what he told us."

A few minutes later Mike, Ian, and Samantha walked down the aisle with Mr. Wonderful. He had been sponged and sheeted, and he was tossing his head and moving easily. He seemed to have come out of the race well.

"Time to take Glory to the saddling paddock," Samantha said.

"We're ready," Cindy said confidently. "I just have to open this." She held up the small white package.

"Who gave you that?" Ian asked.

"Ben Cavell. He came to visit Glory." Cindy carefully separated the tissue paper. "Oh, look!" she gasped, holding up an exquisitely wrought silver bracelet of horses galloping in a circle. "It's so beautiful!" The fluid, endless motion of galloping racehorses was captured perfectly.

Cindy read the card.

To Glory, his and yours. Good luck—I hope this bracelet symbolizes an endless string of victories for him.

Ben Cavell

"Wow, Cindy. The Townsends have never given Ashleigh a bracelet for her riding and training," Samantha teased.

"Brad stopped by just now. He had the usual good things to say." Cindy put on the bracelet. It gleamed softly, almost mysteriously in the muted light of the barn. For a second Cindy thought she saw the silver horses move.

"Maybe Brad really came by to give Ashleigh a present," Ian suggested.

"I don't see it anywhere," Mike said with a laugh.

Cindy led Glory out of his stall and looked him over. She was satisfied with her grooming and exercise work. Glory's coat gleamed like molten metal, as silver as the horses on the bracelet, and his powerful muscles bunched and released as he lightly sidestepped.

Cindy realized she didn't feel nervous anymore. This was a great moment for Glory—what they'd all been working toward at Whitebrook. She'd done all she could. Now it was up to him and Ashleigh.

"We'll see you up in the stands," Beth called to Cindy, waving as she, Ian, Mike, and Samantha walked off down the aisle. Cindy nodded.

The gray colt seemed to know something was up. He whinnied softly as Cindy clipped a lead shank to his halter to take him to the saddling paddock.

The seven other horses in Glory's race were already there with their grooms and trainers. A stiff wind blew from the west, flapping the horses' saddlecloths. Len straightened Glory's special saddlecloth with his name emblazoned on the sides and cinched the light racing saddle to his back.

"Okay, big guy," he said. "I'm counting on you. Mind your manners."

Ashleigh walked over and leaned against the stall partition. She looked preoccupied, as she always did before she rode in a race.

"Ashleigh—" Cindy hesitated.

"Yes?" Ashleigh looked at her.

"If Glory acts up, try talking to him," Cindy said in a rush. "I think he really might need that."

"I usually do talk to the horses I ride, but—" Suddenly Ashleigh looked intently at Cindy, as if something were telling her the race depended on this advice. "Okay," she said. "I'll be sure to talk to him."

Glory was excited now, skittering away from Len, trying to see the other horses walking out to the track. Cindy felt a flicker of nervousness. Would talking to Glory work? That seemed like such a simple answer to a big problem. What if he shied, and Ashleigh or Glory got hurt?

Ashleigh seemed to understand. "Don't worry, Cindy. I honestly don't think Glory can act worse than Wonder sometimes did when she was young. Maybe being sensitive is part of being a champion. I'll hang on tight."

"Do you think he can win it?" Cindy asked. She knew Ashleigh had always been one of Glory's staunchest allies. But she needed to hear again that Ashleigh had confidence in the big gray horse.

"Of course I do," Ashleigh said firmly.

Cindy felt a big lump in her throat. If anyone could win the race with Glory, she knew that person would be Ashleigh. Cindy stroked Glory's satiny neck one last time. "Run fast, boy," she whispered.

Glory stopped his fidgeting and dropped his head to her hands. Cindy closed her eyes for just a second to bask in the familiar nearness of her horse and the feel of his warm breath on her fingers.

"He'll blow by the whole field." Ashleigh smiled and fastened her helmet. Len gave her a leg into the saddle.

"I know," Cindy whispered as Ashleigh rode Glory out of the saddling paddock to the track.

As Cindy pushed through the crowd to get to the grandstand, she noticed on the board that the odds on Glory weren't bad. A Kentucky-bred horse named Azerbaijan was going in as the favorite, but Glory wasn't at the bottom of the heap. Probably most horsepeople knew why he hadn't raced a two-year-old season.

He'll win big, Cindy told herself, climbing to her seat in the stands with her family. *I'm sure of that.* A fat drop plopped on her head. *Now I just wonder if it'll pour.*

Ashleigh rode Glory by the stands in the post parade. Cindy admired the finely bred Thoroughbred almost as if he wasn't hers. With generations of winners in his pedigree, he looked every inch a champion. She saw with relief that the noise and distractions from the stands didn't faze the big colt, even when a paper bag sailed lazily onto the track a few inches from his hooves.

Cindy's stomach calmed a little, then twisted again when Glory balked going into the starting gate. Ashleigh sat quietly. A gate attendant tugged on Glory's bridle, and the colt reluctantly loaded.

A rainbow appeared, arching high over the starting gate and disappearing into the hills. The sky was clearing to the west, turning a pale, clean-washed blue.

"I never saw *that* before at a race," Samantha said, pointing to the rainbow.

"It's a perfect rainbow," Cindy said happily. "Not just a half one, the way they sometimes are."

"I'll bet you're thinking this is an omen that Glory will win." Mike chuckled.

"I know it is," Cindy said, admiring the brilliant colors of the rainbow.

The gate attendants struggled to load the six horse. Finally, with two attendants at the horse's head and two pushing from behind, the horse stepped into the gate. Instantly the bell rang, and eight Thoroughbreds surged into the race.

Glory broke sharply from the gate but angled out wide and dropped back. He seemed content to lag four lengths, then six behind pacesetter Ecstasy, a big black colt. Glory was still ahead of two horses that had collided coming out of the gate, but the rest of the field roared by him.

Cindy squeezed her hands so tightly they hurt. She couldn't believe Glory was so far behind.

Samantha crumpled her program and half rose from her seat. "This is a sprint! He'll lose if he runs that far back! Why is he running so far off the pace?"

Cindy groaned. Frantically her eyes followed Glory's gray coat. The big horse dropped from sixth to seventh, then to dead last. Glory's ears were pricked. "He's not running off the pace!" she cried. "He's scared, and he's not even trying!"

Ashleigh leaned up over Glory's neck, the usual signal to reduce speed.

"What is Ashleigh doing?" Samantha muttered. "She can't be asking him to slow down. He's already going too slow."

In a flash Cindy knew. "She's talking to him." Glory's ears flicked back. "And he's listening!" she said excitedly.

Suddenly Glory gave a tremendous bound. Rapidly he began to pick off the horses in front of him.

"Now he's making his move," Samantha said. "But I don't think he'll have enough time to close!"

Glory was behind a solid wall of four horses, looking for room. Ashleigh seemed to check him, then she leaned forward again. The colt responded with a powerful surge that vaulted him four paths wide and abreast of the leaders.

"Here comes March to Glory into the stretch," the announcer called. "The Whitebrook colt is making his bid for the lead. . . ." Glory began to edge clear.

Azerbaijan, the Kentucky-bred favorite, slipped through along the rail to challenge. But Ashleigh had seen him. So had Glory. Suddenly the colt changed leads and found another gear, pounding farther into the lead.

"Come on, Glory," Cindy screamed. "Put them all away!"

Glory continued to pull ahead, a twelve-hundred-pound blur of solid gray muscle and motion. With fifty yards to go Ashleigh took the colt under a hold.

"Why is she trying to slow him down?" Cindy asked, her heart in her throat. Was something wrong with Glory? Desperately she watched his strides.

"Ashleigh's trying to save him," Samantha exclaimed. "No point in using him up. Why win by a mile? Oh, Cindy, this is incredible!"

But Glory refused to be held back. Dragging the reins through Ashleigh's fingers, he plunged ahead.

"We're going for a new track record," the announcer shouted. "Can the gray colt pull it off? He's charging for the wire . . . he's under it! Here is March to Glory in an absolute shocker. The colt's first race, and he's set a track record in the mud. Ladies and gentlemen, you are present at history in the making!"

"I can't believe it!" Samantha cried. "Cindy, Glory didn't just set a track record. He won his first race by *twenty lengths*!"

"He's the best horse in the world!" Cindy wiped tears of joy from her eyes.

Beth hugged her tight. "Congratulations, honey. You've worked hard for this."

"Looks like Whitebrook has another champion," Ian said happily. "Let's get down to the winner's circle!"

The Whitebrook group pushed through the bedlam on the track to Ashleigh and Glory. Ashleigh dismounted, wiping mud from her face with a handkerchief. "What a romp!" she said, grinning.

The big gray was barely winded. He snorted and pranced, seeming to know just how glorious his achievement had been.

"Oh, Glory," Cindy cried. "You did it, boy. Thank you! I love you so much!"

Cindy hugged Ashleigh, then Glory, then herself. Suddenly Glory shook himself ferociously, sending mud flying into the surrounding group of reporters, photographers, and admirers. A few people cried out in dismay.

"Share in the mud, Cindy." Ashleigh laughed. "Look at you now!"

Cindy saw that in just a few seconds she'd gotten almost as muddy as Glory and Ashleigh. That seemed a badge of honor, under the circumstances.

"I guess I don't need to ask how Glory handled the surface. He's a bulldozer in the mud," Mike said cheerfully.

"How did you get him going?" Cindy asked Ashleigh. She felt dazed with happiness.

"I started talking to him," Ashleigh said. "Just out of the gate too much was going on for me to do it, and he did seem afraid—or at least he wasn't thinking about running. But he snapped out of it. Then his heart and his love of winning took over. Whatever it was, it worked!"

"It sure did!" Ian said.

Ashleigh took Glory's saddle to weigh in. "Glory, you're so dirty you look like a chocolate horse," Cindy told him, smiling so hugely her face hurt.

Ashleigh walked back over to join them. "After today's amazing victory, what's next for this horse?" a reporter yelled.

"Are you looking ahead to Saratoga?" another called.

"Give me a break, everybody," Ashleigh said good-naturedly. "We all had confidence in our horse—but maybe not quite this much! We'll see how he comes out of this race and almost certainly run him this summer. More than that I can't say right now."

"Come on, you guys—pose!" Samantha pushed through the crowd of reporters and photographers to join Ashleigh and Cindy in the winner's circle.

Cindy smiled broadly for the photographers' cameras as she stepped closer to Glory. He rested his head lightly on her shoulder and blew softly into her hair.

"What a shot!" a reporter yelled. Cameras clicked.

"Get good at this, Glory. We're going to be standing in a lot of winner's circles, aren't we?" Cindy said proudly.

The big gray snorted and tossed his head, as if he couldn't agree more.

Joanna Campbell was born and raised in Norwalk, Connecticut and grew up loving horses. She eventually owned a horse of her own and took riding lessons for a number of years, specializing in jumping. She still rides when possible and has started her three-year-old granddaughter on lessons. In addition to publishing over twenty-five novels for young adults, she is the author of four adult novels. She has also sung and played piano professionally and owned an antique business. She now lives on the coast of Maine in Camden with her husband, Ian Bruce. She has two children, Kimberly and Kenneth, and three grand-children

Karen Bentley rode in English equitation and jumping classes as a child and in Western equitation and barrel racing classes as a teenager. She has bred and raised Quarter Horses and, during a sojourn on the East Coast, owned a half-Thoroughbred jumper. She now owns a red roan registered Quarter Horse with some reining moves and lives in New Mexico. She has published four novels for young adults.